Transworld Student

Theoretical Statistics – B

STANLEY N. COLLINGS

Theoretical Statistics does not pretend that statistics is a non-mathematical subject. Starting from a few A-level concepts, and confining itself to discrete situations, it provides a clear introduction to how these concepts are used in formulating the basic ideas upon which probability and sampling notions are built.

Stanley Collings was educated at the Leys School and Emmanuel College, Cambridge. He was Wrangler in 1941 and Senior Scholar of his college. Together with many now well-known names, he learnt his Statistics in a research department under Professor G. A. Barnard. He is now Reader in Statistics at the Open University.

Transworld Student Library is a series of books devoted to topics in Mathematics and the Sciences designed to meet the modern educational needs of the independent learner. The academic level varies with the familiarity of the material covered, from general introductory presentations suitable for sixth-form pupils and school leavers to more specialized topics treated at first- or second-year University level. At the same time, many of the books will be of interest to the general reader with an enquiring mind who wishes to become acquainted with some of the more recent developments in Mathematics and the Sciences.

For the most part, the treatment breaks away from the traditional presentation geared to the classroom situation and provides a refreshingly new approach to the subject matter being discussed.

The criteria for inclusion in the series are that a book shall be clear and understandable in what it has to say; that the academic standard shall be impeccable; that the author shall be genuinely enthusiastic in his desire and ability to communicate to the reader; that the presentation shall be as concise as is compatible with clear understanding; that particular attention shall be paid to the provision of illustrative material; and that the principal aim shall be to stimulate the reader's interest and his desire to study further as well as to provide information and general background material.

Some of the books in the Library are first English translations of outstanding foreign works where these meet the criteria for inclusion, but the majority are specially commissioned from authors who, whilst being specialists in their subjects, are nevertheless prepared to break away from traditional and now outmoded approaches and present their material in a manner consistent with the new adult educational requirements.

Transworld Student Library

General Editor

H. GRAHAM FLEGG, M.A., D.C.Ae., C.Eng., F.I.M.A., M.I.E.E., A.F.R.Ae.S., F.R.Met.S.
Reader in Mathematics, The Open University

Other books in this series
1. *Boolean Algebra*   H. G. Flegg
2. *Theoretical Statistics: Basic Ideas*   S. N. Collings
3. *Points and Arrows: the Theory of Graphs*   A. Kaufmann
4. *Meteorology*   H.-J. Tanck
5. *Field Projects in Sociology*   J. P. Wiseman and M. S. Aron
6. *The Unknown Ego*   T. Brocher
7. *Calculus via Numerical Analysis*   A. Graham and G. Read
8. *Basic Mathematical Structures I*   N. Gowar and H. G. Flegg

Theoretical Statistics
Basic Ideas

by

Stanley N. Collings
Reader in Statistics, The Open University

TRANSWORLD PUBLISHERS LTD
A National General Company
In association with Richard Sadler Ltd

THEORETICAL STATISTICS — BASIC IDEAS

A TRANSWORLD STUDENT LIBRARY BOOK 0 552 40002 5
Originally published in Great Britain
by Macdonald & Co. (Publishers) Ltd.
in the Home Student Library

PRINTING HISTORY
Macdonald edition published 1971
Transworld Student Library edition published 1972
in association with Richard Sadler Ltd.
© Stanley N. Collings 1971

Conditions of sale—This book is sold subject to the
condition that it shall not, by way of trade *or otherwise*,
be lent, re-sold, hired out or otherwise *circulated*
without the publisher's prior consent in any form of
binding or cover other than that in which it is published
*and without a similar condition including this condition
being imposed on the subsequent purchaser.*

Transworld Student Library Books are published by
Transworld Publishers Ltd,
Cavendish House, 57–59 Uxbridge Road, Ealing, London, W.5

Printed in England by
Hazell Watson & Viney Ltd, Aylesbury, Bucks

Contents

1. PROBABILITY
- 1.1 Where It All Begins 1
- 1.2 Random Sequences 4
- 1.3 Attempt at Definition of Probability 6

2. THE SAMPLE SPACE
- 2.1 The Sample Space 8
- 2.2 Probability Models 11
- 2.3 Randomness 13
- 2.4 Events 14

3. THE RULES OF PROBABILITY
- 3.1 Data on a Continuous Scale 18
- 3.2 Rule 1 20
- 3.3 Rule 2 20
- 3.4 Rule 3 21
- 3.5 Rule 4 22
- 3.6 Conditional Probability 23
- 3.7 Definition of Independence 25

4. PROBABILITY PROBLEMS
- 4.1 Introduction 27
- 4.2 Problems and Answers 29

CONTENTS

5. CUMULATIVE DISTRIBUTION FUNCTIONS
- 5.1 Random Variables — 35
- 5.2 The Cumulative Distribution Function — 36
- 5.3 Examples of Cumulative Distribution Functions — 37
- 5.4 Summarising the Properties of C.D.F.'s — 41
- 5.5 Bivariate Distributions — 43
- 5.6 Multivariate Distributions — 44

6. DISCRETE DISTRIBUTIONS
- 6.1 Expectations — 45
- 6.2 Moments — 47
- 6.3 Moments about the Mean — 49
- 6.4 Transformation of Random Variables — 51
- 6.5 More General Transformation — 52
- 6.6 Inequalities Involving Moments of a Distribution — 53
- 6.7 Moment Generating Functions — 55

7. PARTICULAR DISCRETE DISTRIBUTIONS
- 7.1 Die Distribution — 58
- 7.2 Binomial Distribution — 59
- 7.3 Poisson Distribution — 60

8. A LAW OF LARGE NUMBERS
- 8.1 Remarks — 63
- 8.2 Stochastic Limits — 65

9. DISCRETE BIVARIATE DISTRIBUTIONS
- 9.1 Expectations — 67
- 9.2 Moments — 69

    9.3 Correlation   72
    9.4 Correlation as a Measure of Association   77
    9.5 Rank Correlation   77
    9.6 Sums of Independent Random Variables   79

10. RANDOM SAMPLING

    10.1 Discrete Multivariate Distributions   82
    10.2 Random Samples   83
    10.3 Sampling Statistics   84
    10.4 Sampling Moments   86

NOTATION   91

INDEX   92

1. Probability

1.1 Where It All Begins

There is no doubt that *probability* is a sophisticated notion. Compared with geometry (say), which has been known about in some detail since the days of Pythagoras and even earlier, the subject of probability was a very late starter, and understandably so. The point as I see it is that the mind can more readily take to things which are definite. Things which are indefinite in some way are always more difficult to digest and sometimes at first appear to have little value. This is something usually recognised by most schoolteachers, who are able to present equations and strict equalities, but meet with much more resistance when they come on to inequalities, approximations and uncertainties. On the other hand, there is sufficient in the concept of probability for it to have forced itself on our attention. So, let us have a look at these earliest beginnings.

Rudimentary ideas of probability may have been milling around for some time before any systematic attempt was made to deal with the subject. These systematic beginnings came when people engaged in games of chance—namely, cards and dice—and wondered what betting odds should be offered on certain outcomes. In these early days, before probability was properly understood, some ghastly howlers were made in the process; but it was a beginning. With the advantage of hindsight, let us pick out the foundation stone on which probability and its behaviour depend. To do this, let us consider the age-old problem of the penny.

If you toss a penny for yourselves, you will realise that it can come down HEAD or TAIL; and having said this, there is virtually nothing more that you can say about the single *trial* (i.e. a single toss of the coin). You could not foretell what the result was going to

1.1 THEORETICAL STATISTICS

be before it occurred; after the event you likewise cannot foretell what it is going to be on the next occasion. There is complete uncertainty about the outcome of future events. With such lack of knowledge it might strike you that we have no basis for any theory at all. But if you were to toss the penny a large number of times and keep a tally of the number m of heads in n tosses, the *relative frequency* of heads at any stage would be m/n. Plotting m/n against n would give you an angular and erratic form of graph similar to the one shown in figure 1.1.

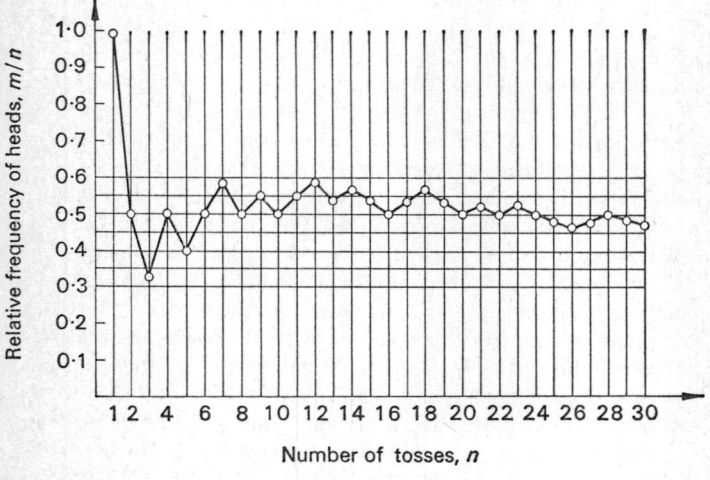

Fig. 1.1

Despite its erratic behaviour, you will notice that the graph has a tendency to converge to a narrow region; and on continuing with the experiment you would find that this region got narrower and narrower. If you are a mathematician, you will probably now be thinking in terms of *the theory of limits*. For example, consider the sequence given by

$$u_n = \tfrac{1}{2} + (-\tfrac{1}{2})^n.$$

This has been plotted in figure 1.2 for various values of n.

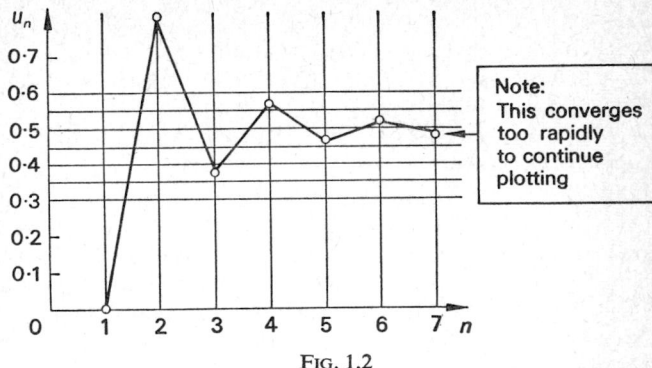

FIG. 1.2

It is clear that this sequence gets nearer and nearer to $\frac{1}{2}$ as n increases, and that in fact it tends to $\frac{1}{2}$ as n tends to infinity. Mathematically we express this by:

$$u_n \to \tfrac{1}{2} \quad \text{as} \quad n \to \infty.$$

As this sequence tends to a limit as n tends to infinity, and as the graph of the relative frequency of heads looks very similar to it in kind, the temptation is to take the relative frequency of heads, to assume that it tends to a limit as n tends to infinity and to call this limiting value of the relative frequency the *probability* of a head. This, after all, is the basic idea behind probability, namely, that it is the relative frequency in the long run as the number of trials increases indefinitely. Whilst we will never disavow these ideas, we cannot proceed in quite this direct manner. But before going into how we do proceed, let us review the progress made so far:

- If an event (e.g. the occurrence of a head) is not certain, it is uncertain.
- When an event is uncertain, no firm prediction is possible.
- With the tossing of a penny, it is an experimental fact that

1.2 THEORETICAL STATISTICS

the relative frequency gets more and more stable as the number of tosses increases.
- This relative frequency has all the appearances of tending to a limit. If we knew that the relative frequency did tend to a limit, we would call the value of that limit the *probability* of the original event.

1.2 Random Sequences

With our penny we took note of the heads which occurred. We could have done this by marking down a 1 every time we got a head, and a 0 every time we got a tail. By this means we would have obtained a sequence of 0's and 1's. My earlier statement amounts to saying that the relative frequency of 1's becomes more and more stable as the number of terms increases, and that this fact gives rise to our initial concepts of probability.

At this point, you might wonder whether all sequences of 0's and 1's behave in this way. The answer clearly is *no*, for consider

$$0110001111110 \ldots.$$

After three terms the relative frequency of 1's is $\frac{2}{3}$.
After six terms it is $\frac{1}{3}$.
After twelve terms it is $\frac{2}{3}$, and etc.

In other words, it is possible to construct a sequence in which the relative frequency does not tend to a limit. So we now ask: what is the difference between this sequence and the one we obtained with the penny? The essential difference is that with our constructed sequence there is a rule for determining what the next term shall be (a rule designed to make the relative frequency oscillate), whereas with the penny the outcome is always quite unpredictable. It is an experimental fact, however, that such sequences of unpredictable outcomes behave as if the relative frequency were tending to a limit.

The unpredictability goes even further than this. For example, you might ask whether, on taking alternate terms, any degree of pattern might emerge. Alternatively, you could look at each term which immediately followed a 0 and ask whether the sub-sequence they formed was in any sense special. In both cases, the answer is *no*, a fact which you can verify for yourselves if you have the patience. In short, the sequence of 0's and 1's is truly devoid of pattern or predictability. Such sequences are said to be *random*.

This does not amount to a formal definition of randomness. It is a little imprecise, and it is expressed in terms of what randomness is not, rather than in terms of what it is. Nevertheless, these negative properties are an essential part of the idea of randomness.

Coming back to our experiment with the penny, what we are saying, in fact, is that the relative frequency of heads will become stable in the long run because the sequence in question is random. But even this has its difficulties. While in the experiment which I plotted, I obtained the kind of results I expected, the awkward fact remains that it would have been perfectly possible for every single result to have been a head. Indeed, if this were not possible, the sequence would not have been random, for it would mean that at a certain stage a tail could be predicted. But for us a random sequence is never predictable.

At this point, you might say: 'Of course, it is possible to get 30 1's in a row; but this is so unlikely that it can be ignored.' This is true enough; but, in expressing these thoughts, you have used the word 'unlikely', which is simply a synonym of 'improbable'. If we are trying to define *probability* in rigorous terms, we must not use another word meaning the same thing in the definition.

Let us summarise where this section has got us:

- The sequence of 0's and 1's obtained in practice from the tossing of a penny (or by other similar means) produces a relative frequency of 1's which becomes more and more stable as the experiment is continued.
- Not all sequences of 0's and 1's have this property. In particular, not some of those which are produced artificially.
- The essential features of such a sequence produced experimentally are that the terms are unpredictable at any stage, and that there is no observable pattern either in the sequence

itself or in any sub-sequence taken from it. (But clearly we must not cheat here by looking at the values of the terms first, and then deliberately choosing, say, all the 1's, or else 0's and 1's alternatively. In other words, the selection or non-selection of a term for the sub-sequence must not depend on the value of that term.)
- These patternless sequences are said to be random.
- Even random sequences of 0's and 1's could produce a run of 1's only, though the longer the run the more unlikely it is to occur by chance only.

1.3 Attempt at Definition of Probability

We have thought of probability in terms of the *limiting value* of a relative frequency. We have observed that not all sequences of 0's and 1's have relative frequencies which tend to any sort of limit. Basing ourselves on background experience, we have accepted that random sequences do have relative frequencies which 'tend to a limit'. Perhaps by now, therefore, we are in a position to formulate a definition of *probability*.

One difficulty still facing us is something we have already encountered. Namely, that however long a sequence may go on, it is always possible to get an unending run of heads. If there is no certainty, then we cannot have a limit in the ordinary mathematical sense of the word. To make quite sure of this, let us look again at the mathematical sequence mentioned earlier, namely,

$$u_n = \tfrac{1}{2} + (-\tfrac{1}{2})^n.$$

In this case, it is *certain* that for all values of $n \geqslant 2$, u_n is within a distance $\tfrac{1}{4}$ of $\tfrac{1}{2}$. For all $n \geqslant 10$, it is *certain* that u_n is within a distance $\tfrac{1}{1024}$ of $\tfrac{1}{2}$, and so forth.

In our case of the penny, however, nothing is certain at all (if it were we would not have randomness). If we cannot have certainty, then we cannot have a mathematical limit. If we cannot have a mathematical limit, we clearly cannot define probability in terms of a limit.

If it is not certain that every random relative frequency tends to a limit, it may still be true that some of them do. Unfortunately, this is not a situation which can ever be tested. However often we toss a penny, the total number of times will always be finite; we have to come to a stop somewhere. But as soon as we come to a stop, we fail to meet the requirements of a mathematical limit.

We are still therefore unable to provide a proper definition of probability or, for that matter, any completely accurate method of assessing the magnitude of a probability, whether we can define it or not. This is not something, however, which need seriously worry us. Few of us could define in adequate philosophical terms what was meant by *distance*, on the other hand all of us know what we mean by *a mile*. Further even than this, we are confident in practice about the concept of a mile, although we would be hard put to have to measure one to very close accuracy. If we tried to measure a distance of a mile on more than one occasion we would almost certainly get slightly different answers each time. If we descended to the atomic scale, we could seriously doubt what we meant by a distance at all as the atoms of the substance being measured would be in a perpetual state of flux. All of this is true; but it does not worry us. In very much the same way, we need not worry about probabilities if we are more interested in applications than in fine philosophical distinctions.

2. The Sample Space

Suppose we have succeeded in defining probability, i.e. in saying what probability is in practical terms. In this case, we would be able—subject possibly to experimental error—to say what the value of a probability was in any particular case. In fact, we have failed. But this does not prevent us from continuing for the time being by giving probabilities numerical values. Before we do this, we first have to consider the *outcomes* or *events* which are going to carry these probabilities. This is where the *sample space* comes in.

2.1 The Sample Space

You might have a wheel (figure 2.1) which is balanced so that it can rotate freely in a vertical plane. If the wheel is perfectly balanced, and there is no unevenness in the bearings, the wheel is equally likely to come to rest in any position. (We have to suppose here that there is a distinguishing point on the wheel which does not disturb its balance.) To test the situation, one obvious procedure is to spin the wheel and to note the angle at which this marker comes to rest on some scale; the final angle could be anything between $0°$ and $360°$. If you were to do this many times you would get a set of values which could be represented by

$$x_1, x_2, \ldots, x_n.$$

You thus have a collection of values, and any argument you use about the balance of the wheel will depend on this or some similar collection.

Just as diagrams help one to see what is going on, so geometrical representations of situations can assist likewise. As soon as we have n separate values like this, we can immediately think of that point

THE SAMPLE SPACE 2.1

P in a space of n dimensions having co-ordinates $x_1, x_2, \ldots, x_n$. For simplicity at this stage, however, we shall take $n = 3$. One immediate advantage of the geometrical representation is that a collection of three separate values has been compounded into one single event, namely the point P. As each x in turn can take any value between 0 and 360 (in degrees), the point P can lie anywhere in a cube of side 360. In other words, P can lie anywhere in a certain space. The set of values x_1, x_2 and x_3 is called a sample (we shall return to this very important topic later on but in slightly different terms) and so it is fair to refer to the cube as a *sample space*.

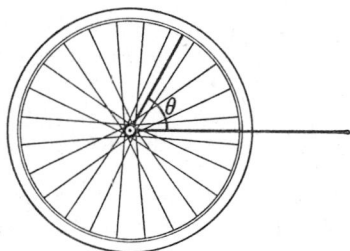

FIG. 2.1

Outcomes of experiments need not be measurements on a continuous scale; they can be perfectly discrete events, such as the 'two of hearts' or the 'king of clubs' when cards are selected from a pack. It is still convenient, however, to use the expression sample space in this case as well. In other words, we can define a sample space as the set of all possible outcomes of some trial whatever form the outcomes may take.

Although it is usually useful to consider all the possible different outcomes which could arise, it is not always so. In some card games (for example, poker) you might be trying to collect THREE OF A KIND, say three 8's. If you have the 'eight of spades' and the 'eight of hearts', then to complete three of a kind you need the 'eight of diamonds' or the 'eight of clubs'—it is immaterial which. Although, therefore, the drawing of the 'eight of diamonds' and the 'eight of

2.1 THEORETICAL STATISTICS

clubs' are two different outcomes, as far as you are concerned from the practical point of view there is no difference. In dice games it is often the rule that you cannot begin until you have thrown a 'six'. In this case, you are interested only in whether the number is a 'six' or not. A 'five' is no good to you, and from your point of view is no different in its effect from a 'four', 'three', 'two' or 'one'. In your position, therefore, the relevant sample space is not the six outcomes, 'one', 'two', 'three', 'four', 'five', 'six', but simply the two points 'six' and 'not-six'. For computational reasons, you may wish to distinguish between the numbers 1 to 5, but that is another question.

Having got a sample space, it remains to ascribe probabilities to the various points in the sample space. We shall now consider this problem in a sample space consisting of a finite number of discrete outcomes.

Commencing with the tossing of a penny, we have to ascribe a number to the outcome HEAD and to the outcome TAIL. The very word 'ascribe' implies a certain arbitrariness about our choice; but it is not as arbitrary as all that. After all, in the long run, we are identifying probability in our mind with relative frequencies so we have to be sure that the figures we ascribe behave in the same way as relative frequencies do. If in any n tosses a coin comes down heads m times, then it will come down tails $(n - m)$ times; the relative frequencies of heads and tails are therefore m/n and $(n - m)/n$, and these two relative frequencies sum to 1. Therefore when we ascribe probabilities to heads and to tails we must be sure that the two values add up to 1 also. But this still leaves quite a choice.

In fact, we know something about coins already from our general experience; in particular, we know that they are (roughly) symmetrical. We may also have tossed them a number of times in the past and seen that the proportion of heads is never far removed from $\frac{1}{2}$, and indeed appeared to get closer to this value as the number of tosses increased. In this situation, we would surely not be reluctant to ascribe the value $\frac{1}{2}$ to the probability of getting a head. In acting in this way, you are not staking your life on your accuracy; you are only settling on a provisional starting point for subsequent work. The true value in a particular case might be ·495; but, if so, you are

THE SAMPLE SPACE 2.2

not going to discover this without a very prolonged experiment, so you are virtually stuck with the value ·5 whether you like it or not. In any case, ·5 could well be close enough to meet the purposes you have in mind. Some people would argue indefinitely about whether to accept ·5 as the true value, in which case they would never make any progress with the subject. Up to a point, it is as if Newton could not decide whether gravitation varied as d^{-2} or $d^{-1\cdot 9}$, and because of this never continued with his mathematics giving the orbit for a gravitational body. It is quite evident that Newton had the right idea; he took the plunge on the value -2, worked out the consequences of this, and then checked these consequences against later observations. This should be our approach also; we should be prepared to ascribe probabilities, to work out consequences of these values, and then to check later.

Pennies have been simple things to deal with because of their symmetry, and because of our general experience of them. There are situations, however, where no single probability obviously suggests itself and where we are utterly reliant on a long sequence of trials for deciding what probability to take. This could happen, for example, with a biased die. In this situation, unless you adopt subjective probability (which we shall not discuss), you simply have to throw the die many times and decide upon a reasonable sort of figure. For example, if you threw it 600 times, and you got a six in 121 of them, you could then assume the probability of a head was $\frac{121}{600}$. A more reasonable thing to do in this case would be to accept a figure of ·2 for working purposes.

2.2 Probability Models

There is one very good reason why we need not get obsessed about the exactness of our guesses for the ascribed value of any probability, and that is that a fair amount of statistical theory is concerned *not* with the true probability of some outcome but with what would follow if the probability were some particular value. For example, at some stage or other in any probability argument we are bound to ask something like: 'If the probability of tossing a head is $\frac{1}{2}$, what is the probability of getting at least two heads out of five

2.2 THEORETICAL STATISTICS

tosses?' You will notice that here we are asking a purely *deductive* question. Nobody has said that the probability of getting a head *is* $\frac{1}{2}$; all we have said is '*if* the probability is $\frac{1}{2}$ ...'. We could equally have said: 'If the probability of a head is ·495, what is the probability of getting at least two heads out of five tosses?' It is obvious that the argument in the two cases will be of identical form, and it is the form of this argument which interests us here.

In any practical situation we can never be sure that the true probability equals the value we have ascribed to it. We might for that matter have grounds for suspecting that the outcome of one trial somehow affects the probabilities for succeeding trials. (The face of a die might get sticky or worn.) These are all questions concerned with the *inductive* side. In our work, implicitly if not explicitly, we have supposed with the tossing of a penny or the throwing of a die that the outcome on one occasion does not affect the probability on succeeding occasions. If this assumption is correct—fine! The point for us at the moment, however, is that there is an assumption here ... not necessarily a particularly wild assumption, but an assumption for all that! If we knew enough about the situation, we might not need to make any assumption; we would know. But if we knew everything we wanted to know, why are we carrying out an experiment at all?

The fact remains that we do not always know everything we want to know, so we have to make some kind of working assumption at some stage to enable us to carry on with the analysis. In the coin case, for example, where we use the relative frequency of heads to check on the value of the probability of a head, we are assuming that the probability is constant throughout the whole experiment. A very reasonable assumption, but, I say, still an assumption! In other words, we are supposing that the physical situation corresponds to what we have assumed; or, to put the whole thing the other way round, we have set up a *probability model* representing the physical situation as far as we can tell.

With something more complicated than a penny it is easier to see the effect of any particular model. With a die, for instance, we would not hesitate to assume in the first place that the probabilities for each of the numbers 1 to 6 were all equal. This is an assumption, or, in our new nomenclature, a *probability model* of the situation.

As statisticians then, we are often concerned with the question of what the consequences would be if a certain model was correct. For example, assuming the probability of a 'six' is $\frac{1}{6}$, what is the probability you would have to throw a die ten times before you got a 'six'? This is *deductive* logic which is essentially a branch of mathematics. (As long as we are engaged on this question, we do not have to worry in the slightest about whether the probability of a 'six' is really $\frac{1}{6}$ or not.) On the other hand, we are sometimes concerned with whether the model itself is correct. For example, is the probability of getting a 'six' $\frac{1}{6}$? This is essentially an *inductive* problem. Funnily enough, we may have to use a good deal of deductive logic in the process of trying to settle the matter.

2.3 Randomness

We first came across the concept of randomness in the context of random sequences of 0's and 1's; these sequences were considered as a prelude to probability. We observed that not all sequences of 0's and 1's had relative frequencies which appeared to tend to a limit, but that random sequences did. In other words, we had to deal with randomness before we dealt with probability, and it was partly because of these difficulties and the circular argument they engendered that we could not provide a formal definition of *probability*.

We cut the Gordian knot by ascribing probabilities to the various possible outcomes, thereby by-passing the question of any formal definition. Having reached *probability* by this method, we are now able to go backwards as it were and provide a formal definition of *randomness*. If we have some physical situation such as the tossing of a coin which provides a sequence of 0's and 1's, and this operation is such that the probability of a 1 at any stage is always the same fixed value, then the sequence is said to be *random*.

Let us see how this definition of randomness squares up with our initial notions on the subject. From its definition, which is expressed entirely in terms of probabilities, we would not expect any pattern

2.4 THEORETICAL STATISTICS

to emerge. Any form of pattern contains a degree of regularity, which means that 1 is going to be predictable in some of the places, and this runs counter to our definition, where the probability is always some fixed p. It follows from this that we expect the absence of pattern already referred to in Chapter 1. In addition, however, the definition of randomness would lead us to expect the right relative frequency of 1's. In fact, the relative frequency of 1's in the long run should equal the probability mentioned in the definition.

2.4 Events

We have introduced the idea of a sample space so as to specify all possible outcomes; we have later ascribed probabilities to these

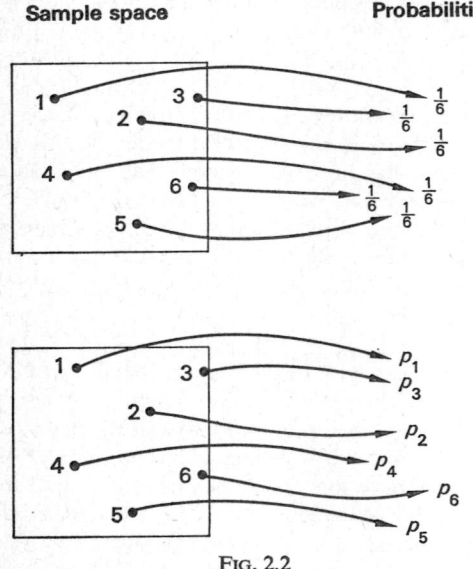

Fig. 2.2

individual outcomes. The diagrams in figure 2.2 show sample spaces with probabilities attached for the throwing of a die; the

14

THE SAMPLE SPACE 2.4

first diagram represents throwing a fair die, and the second a loaded die whose probabilities are not initially known.

You will notice that there is a mapping from the individual outcomes to the probabilities attached to them. In the first case, each point maps to the value $\frac{1}{6}$; in the second the rth point maps to the value p_r. As these latter probabilities are initially unknown, we will at some stage have the task of ascribing values to the unknowns $p_1, p_2, \ldots, p_6$.

In some situations we are concerned not with the individual outcomes themselves but with the combinations of them. For example, with the fair die we might be interested in whether the outcome was an odd number or an even number. In this case, we are not directly interested in the separate probabilities of a 1, 3, or 5, but in the probability of one or other of these. You would perhaps argue intuitively that the probability of getting an odd number was equal to $\frac{1}{6} + \frac{1}{6} + \frac{1}{6} = \frac{1}{2}$. You would be correct. In the second diagram you would equally argue that the probability was $p_1 + p_3 + p_5$. This also is correct; but let us see what is involved. First of all, we are concerned not directly with individual points in the sample space but with sets or combinations of them. Such combinations are subsets of the whole sample space; we therefore give a special name to such a subset and call it an *event*.

> **Definition:** An *event* is a subset of all possible outcomes in a sample space.

The subsets can be of any form. On the one hand, a subset could consist of the whole sample space; on the other, it could be empty. In between, a subset would consist of some but not all the sample points.

Returning to our problem of the odd numbers, what we have to do is to settle what probability should be ascribed to the event '1 or 3 or 5'. This is represented in the diagram in figure 2.3.

To answer this question we must go back to fundamentals, i.e. to what probability means to us. We have previously associated it

2.4 THEORETICAL STATISTICS

with relative frequency. Suppose therefore that we carried out n trials (n large), and that in the course of these trials 1 came up m_1 times, 3 came up m_3 times and 5 came up m_5 times. Then, because of the relationship between relative frequency and probability, we would expect m_1/n to be close to p_1, m_3/n to be close to p_3 and m_5/n to be close to p_5.

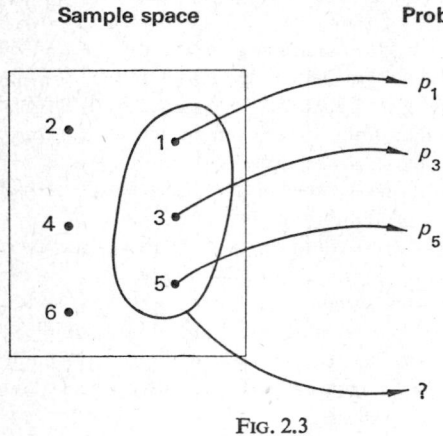

Fig. 2.3

The relative frequency with which an odd number has come up is clearly equal to $(m_1 + m_3 + m_5)/n$, and we would expect this value to be close to what we want, namely, the probability of getting an odd number. But

$$\frac{m_1 + m_3 + m_5}{n} = \frac{m_1}{n} + \frac{m_3}{n} + \frac{m_5}{n}$$

which is close to $p_1 + p_3 + p_5$. This indicates that the probability to be ascribed to our event is obtained by *addition* of the individual probabilities concerned.

This *addition rule* can be applied in a more general way still. Suppose we have a sample space consisting of individual points, and

THE SAMPLE SPACE 2.4

suppose that in this sample space we have two events A and B which have no points in common. Events (or subsets) which have no common point are said to be *exclusive*. By addition—as in the previous paragraph—we can find the probability of getting the event A; this can be represented by $P(A)$. Similarly, we have $P(B)$. An event consisting of all points which are in A or B is called the *union* of A and B. This is denoted by $A \cup B$*. To get the probability of $A \cup B$, we add together the probabilities of the separate sample points in $A \cup B$. These sample points fall into two distinct classes—those belonging to A (and their probabilities add to $P(A)$) and those belonging to B (and their probabilities add to $P(B)$). In other words

$$P(A \cup B) = P(A) + P(B).$$

This is known as the addition rule for exclusive events (figure 2.4).

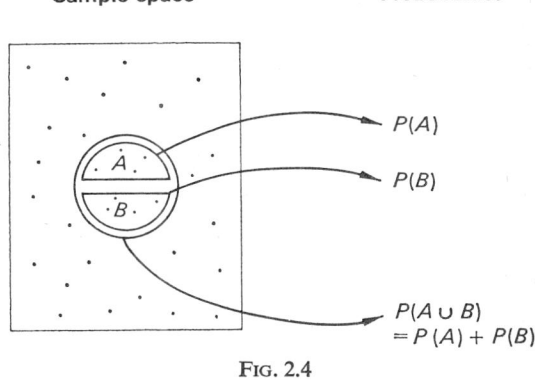

Fig. 2.4

* For a fuller discussion of set algebra and notation see *Boolean Algebra* by H. Graham Flegg; Home Student Library, Macdonald, 1971.

3. The Rules of Probability

3.1 Data on a Continuous Scale

When we had discrete data, particularly with only a finite number of possible outcomes, it was easy to consider each outcome in turn, to ascribe a probability to each outcome, and to sum the ascribed probabilities making sure that this was equal to 1. The situation with discrete data having an infinite number of outcomes is a little different, but not essentially so. For example, we could count how many throws of a die were necessary before we got a six. A six could turn up on the first throw, or on the second throw or not until the third, or not until the fourth and so on. This progression could be unending, and in a sense we might not get a six until we have thrown an infinite number of times. The difference in this case is that instead of adding together a finite number of terms we have to take the sum of an infinite series.

With continuous data the position is more difficult. Suppose, for example, that we have two wheels—one of a standard construction and one made in some special way. We could carry out an experiment under which we rotated each of them, so as to see where each of them came to rest. If each wheel had a distinguishing mark on it, we could measure the stopping position by knowing the angle (in degrees) made by the mark; this angle would be θ, where θ lies between 0 and 360. With two wheels, we would have θ_1 for the standard wheel, and θ_2 for the special wheel. We could then represent the result of the whole experiment by a point P whose coordinates were θ_1, θ_2. Such a point would lie in a square of side 360. The question could arise as to the probability of P lying in a specified area. Anything we say about probability must ultimately be applicable to this situation as well. When we first meet *continuity* in calculus, it is usual to consider small discrete values. For example, when we first investigate the area underneath a curve, we divide the area into a set of narrow rectangles, usually of width δx or something equivalent. In our case, we break down the whole continuous square into a number of very small rectangles of sides δx_1 and δx_2. Each rectangle is a subset of the whole sample space; it is therefore an event as defined in Chapter 2. We thus have a finite set of discrete events building up to a whole sample space. If we are now interested in whether the point P lies in some particular finite region (as opposed to infinitesimal region) of the sample space, all we need do is to take all the infinitesimal rectangles making up the region concerned (see figure 3.1).

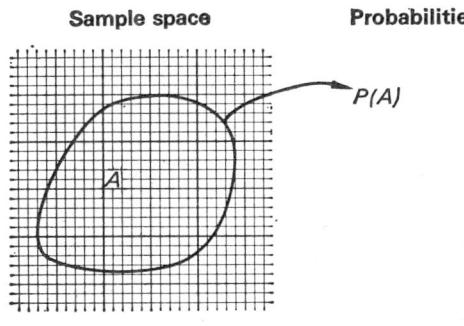

Fig. 3.1

This explains in a formal way how we would deal with continuous data, and how we would set about working out the probability that the sample point P lay in some particular region. All we need know, however, for our general purposes is that associated with any region there will be a probability. Each region, being a subset of the sample space, is an event; hence associated with any event A will be a probability represented by $P(A)$.

We have progressed from probabilities of particular discrete outcomes to the probabilities of more complicated events determined by regions in a continuous sample space. Are there any rules

3.2 THEORETICAL STATISTICS

which such probabilities in their new form have to obey? There are, and some of them can already be guessed from the remarks made earlier. It will be convenient at this stage to consider such rules under headings.

3.2 Rule 1

> For any event A, $0 \leqslant P(A) \leqslant 1$.
> $P(A) = 0$ if A is *impossible*.
> $P(A) = 1$ if A is *certain*.

The first line here should be perfectly acceptable. As probabilities are associated in our minds with relative frequencies which are certainly greater than or equal to 0, and cannot exceed 1, then probabilities are bound to have the same property.

If an event is impossible, it will never occur, however many trials are carried out. The relative frequency of occurrence will always be 0; we would therefore expect the probability of an impossible event to be zero. Rule 1 therefore merely formalises what is already familiar and acceptable.

The same remarks apply to events which are certain. If A is certain, it will occur on every occasion; the relative frequency will therefore be 1 always. We should therefore be prepared to accept that $P(A) = 1$.

Having stated this rule, it is natural to enquire whether the converse is true. That is, if $P(A) = 0$, is A impossible? The answer is *no*, though the reason is more easily seen if we have studied continuous distributions. We can appreciate the kind of thing involved if we consider an infinite plane and a single drop of rain. Because the plane is of infinite size, the probability that the drop of rain falls in any particular position is zero, yet it is still possible.

3.3 Rule 2

If to a trial there are n possible outcomes, and these are equally likely, then the probability that one or other of a subset of m of them will occur is equal to m/n.

This rule applies purely to the finite discrete situation. Its truth is intuitively obvious, but justification can be provided as follows. As all outcomes are equally likely, each outcome has probability p (say). If S is the sample space,

$1 = P(S)$, as S is certain.
$= p + p + \ldots + p$ (to n terms)
$= np$.

[We add the p's as the individual outcomes are exclusive.]

Therefore, $p = 1/n$. Therefore, by addition once again, the probability that one or other of a subset m occurs is

$$p + p + \ldots + p \quad \text{(to } m \text{ terms)}$$
$$= mp$$
$$= m/n.$$

This is intuitively so obvious that one might wonder why the result has been incorporated as a rule. The answer is that it is a formula which is used many times, and to make it a rule helps to fix it as a reference point.

3.4 Rule 3

If A and B are *exclusive* events then

$$P(A \cup B) = P(A) + P(B)$$

If we broke down the continuous sample space into infinitesimal discrete events, then by the arguments of the last chapter, the exclusive events A and B would have no infinitesimal region in common; therefore the probabilities are additive. This result remains true when we deal with the continuous regions made up by our infinitesimal rectangles.

In all our work above, we have been thinking of the sample space consisting of a square of side 360. But this has been just to fix our ideas. In fact, the rules quoted apply in the most general situation. For example, if the sample space were of some other shape or of infinite size, or were in any number of dimensions.

3.5 THEORETICAL STATISTICS

3.5 Rule 4

Suppose I draw two cards at random from a full pack of 52 cards (excluding the joker), and that I am interested in their both being aces. One way of proceeding is to argue:

> The probability that the first is an ace is $\frac{4}{52}$. This leaves 51 cards in the pack of which three are aces. The probability that the second card is now an ace is $\frac{3}{51}$. Therefore the probability that both are aces is $\frac{4}{52} \times \frac{3}{51} = \frac{1}{221}$.

You may accept this argument as it stands. If you cannot, the following remarks may help. There is no trouble at all about the $\frac{4}{52}$, nor about the $\frac{3}{51}$ as being the probability of the second card. The only possible doubt arises over the multiplication sign. But if we think in terms of relative frequency, we observe immediately that on repeating the whole experiment many times, in $\frac{4}{52}$ of them we shall have an ace on the first occasion, and that in each of these successful instances only a proportion of $\frac{3}{51}$ will have the second card an ace. We have therefore a proportion of a proportion, namely, $\frac{3}{51}$ of $\frac{4}{52}$, and this is $\frac{3}{51} \times \frac{4}{52} = \frac{1}{221}$.

An alternative way of doing the whole thing is to consider the two cards being drawn simultaneously; in this case, we count the number of possible pairs. Applying the standard result in combination theory (see footnote*), this is $\binom{52}{2}$. By random shuffling, all these pairs are equally likely. The number of these pairs consisting of two aces is simply the number of ways of drawing two aces from four; by the same argument this is $\binom{4}{2}$. Therefore, by Rule 2, the

---

*$\binom{n}{r}$ is a binomial coefficient. It is sometimes written ^nC_r, and it is the coefficient of x^r in the expansion of $(1 + x)^n$. It can be shown that

$$\binom{n}{r} = \frac{n(n-1)(n-2)(n-3)\ldots 2.1}{r(r-1)\ldots 2.1.(n-r)(n-r-1)\ldots 2.1}$$
$$= \frac{n!}{r!(n-r)!}$$

probability that the pair of cards consists of two aces is $\binom{4}{2}/\binom{52}{2}$, and this works out to $\frac{1}{221}$. Argue it out how you like, we always get the same answer. What I want to draw attention to is that we get the right answer by multiplying the two probability values. This can be expressed better in symbolic terms. If A and B are two events, the probability they *both* occur is given by the formula

P (both A and B) $= P(A \cap B)$ [using set notation]

$= P(A) \times P(B/\text{given } A \text{ has occurred}) = P(B/A)$.

$P(B/A)$ is standard notation for the expression 'the probability of B given that A has occurred'. We therefore finish up with the rule

$$P(A \cap B) = P(A).P(B/A)$$

If $P(A) = 0$, it is obvious that $P(A \cap B) = 0$. We therefore do not need to apply any rule to get the answer. It would in any case be rather a waste of time speculating on what the probability of B would be if A were to occur when A is not expected to occur at all. To regularise this situation, we shall refer to the conditional probability $P(B/A)$ only when $P(A) \neq 0$. Put another way, if we write '$P(B/A)$', we are tacitly assuming that $P(A) \neq 0$.

3.6 Conditional Probability

In Rule 4 we come across the notion of a *conditional probability* for the first time. Let us think about this a little more deeply. In the card experiment, the probability that the second card was an ace was quoted as being $\frac{3}{51}$. This was a conditional probability, the condition being that the first card was an ace. Even if the first card was not an ace, we would still have a condition because we would be drawing from 51 cards and not from 52.

Recapitulating:

- If we did not draw an earlier card, the probability of getting an ace is $\frac{4}{52}$.

3.6 THEORETICAL STATISTICS

- If we did draw a card earlier, the probability of drawing an ace is a conditional probability; this equals $\frac{3}{51}$ (if the first card was an ace) and $\frac{4}{51}$ (if the first card was not). In neither case is the conditional probability equal to $\frac{4}{52}$ (which might be called the *unconditional* probability).

Take a situation from life. Suppose a shot-putter is trying to achieve 55 ft. It is uncertain on any occasion that he will do so. It may be reasonable to say that he has a probability of, say, $\frac{1}{3}$ of doing so. To increase his chances of success, he decides to take some drug to build up his body strength, but he does not take it on every occasion. If I were to ask you, 'What is the probability he throws more than 55 ft?', you might well reply, 'Has he taken the drug or hasn't he?' In other words, in this situation it is the conditional probability which is the most relevant figure. If he has taken the drug, what we want to know is the probability that he throws 55 ft *given* that he has taken it. The athlete obviously imagines that the drug is going to do him good; in other words, the conditional probability that he throws 55 ft given that he has taken the drug is more than $\frac{1}{3}$ (at least in his mind).

We can also exhibit conditional probabilities with a die. I may throw a die, and have a bet with one person that event A will occur, and have a bet with another person that event B will occur. Suppose that A is the event of getting the number X, where $X = 1$ or 2 or 3 or 4, and suppose B is the event $X = 3$ or 4; then

$$P(A) = \tfrac{2}{3}$$
$$P(B) = \tfrac{1}{3}.$$

But consider the probability of B occurring knowing that event A has occurred. In this case, X can only be 1 or 2 or 3 or 4, and it is equally likely to take any of these four values. Two of these values make B occur and two do not. Therefore, the conditional probability that B occurs given that A occurs is $\frac{2}{4} = \frac{1}{2}$. Recapitulating, we have

$$P(B) = \tfrac{1}{3}$$
$$P(B/A) = \tfrac{1}{2}.$$

Suppose, however, that we change A to the event

$$X = 1 \text{ or } 2 \text{ or } 3.$$

Now if A occurs, the number on the die must be 1 or 2 or 3; only one of these values makes B occur, therefore the probability of B given that A has occurred is $\frac{1}{3}$. In other words,

$$P(B/A) = \tfrac{1}{3} = P(B).$$

In this case, therefore, the conditional probability is equal in value to the unconditional probability. It makes no difference to the probability of B whether A has occurred or not. In other words, B is, in a sense, independent of A.

We have adopted the word 'independent', which could be a dangerous thing to do as it means so much to us already in other contexts. Is the usage fair? Before answering this, let us go back to our shot-putter. If in his case it was found by experiment that the conditional probability of throwing 55 ft was still equal to $\frac{1}{5}$, any reasonable man would say that the drug had no effect; so they could also say that his performance was independent of the drug. But this is all we are saying with our die; that if the probability of some event is not affected by the occurrence of some earlier event then the second event is independent of the first. So although the word 'independent' has been applied purely in a probability situation, it adequately expresses what is at stake. (If you were to see this more easily with the shot-putter than with the die, I would not quibble; but it really does come down to the same thing.)

3.7 Definition of Independence

Arising out of our consideration of conditional probability, we come across the notion of one event being independent of another. There is, however, more to be said about the situation, though we need mathematics to show it. We are saying that B is independent of A if $P(B/A) = P(B)$.

But $\qquad P(A \cap B) = P(A).P(B/A) \qquad\qquad$ Rule 4

3.7 THEORETICAL STATISTICS

Therefore, $\quad P(A \cap B) = P(A).P(B).\quad$ by substitution

Conversely if $\quad P(A \cap B) = P(A).P(B),\quad$ given

$$P(A \cap B) = P(A).P(B/A) \quad \text{Rule 4}$$

Therefore, $\quad P(B/A) = P(B)$ for, tacitly, $P(A) \neq 0$.

Thus to say $\quad P(B/A) = P(B)$ is equivalent to saying

$$P(A \cap B) = P(A).P(B), \text{ and conversely.}$$

Therefore, we could adopt either as our formal definition of independence. We strongly prefer the latter, because it is symmetrical in A and B, which implies immediately that independence is a mutual property; i.e. that if B is independent of A, then A is independent of B. As this now works either way round, all we need say in future is that 'A and B are independent'. If you prefer not to rely on symmetry arguments, you can quickly prove for yourself that $P(B/A) = P(B)$ implies $P(A/B) = P(A)$.

When we said that the two statements about independence were equivalent, there was in fact one slight qualification; the use of the expression $P(B/A)$ implied that $P(A)$ was not zero. To keep the two statements completely in line, we do not define independence when $P(A)$ or $P(B)$ is zero. It may still be true that $P(A \cap B) = P(A).P(B)$ (indeed if you think about it, you will realise that it must be true); but we just do not use the *word* 'independent' in this very special case.

In conclusion, therefore, we adopt as our formal definition of independence:

A and B are independent if

$$P(A \cap B) = P(A).P(B) \neq 0.$$

If

$$P(A \cap B) \neq P(A).P(B),$$

A and B are said to be dependent.

4. Probability Problems

4.1 Introduction

One wants elementary probability as much as anything to solve problems. Before tackling these, let us clear one or two formalities out of the way.

(1) If A' represents the event 'not-A', then the events A and A' are exhaustive (they exhaust all possibilities between them), and so

$A \cup A'$ is certain.

Therefore, $1 = P(A \cup A')$ Rule 1

$\qquad = P(A) + P(A').$ Rule 3 as A and A' are exclusive

Therefore, $P(A') = 1 - P(A).$

This is as we would expect; but at least we have proved it!

(2) If A, B, C are all mutually exclusive then A and $B \cup C$ are exclusive,

Therefore, $P(A \cup B \cup C) = P\{A \cup (B \cup C)\}$

$\qquad = P(A) + P(B \cup C)$ Rule 3

$\qquad = P(A) + P(B) + P(C).$ Rule 3

Similarly, for four mutually exclusive events,

$P(A \cup B \cup C \cup D) = P(A) + P(B) + P(C) + P(D)$, etc.

(3) By definition, events A and B are both subsets of some sample space S. A part of A may overlap with B, and we can represent this by $X = A \cap B$. The remainder of A will overlap with B',

4.1 THEORETICAL STATISTICS

and we can represent this by $Y = A \cap B'$. Then X and Y are clearly exclusive.

Also together they make up the whole of A; i.e.

$$A = X \cup Y$$

Therefore, $\quad P(A) = P(X \cup Y)$
$\qquad\qquad\quad = P(X) + P(Y) \qquad\qquad$ Rule 3
$\qquad\qquad\quad = P(A \cap B) + P(A \cap B').$

Therefore, $P(A \cap B') = P(A) - P(A \cap B)$.

These arguments still apply even if X or Y are empty.

(4) Sample points lying in $C = A \cup B$ lie in A or in B or in both. Points of C lying in B clearly form the set B. Points of C not lying in B must lie in A; also not lying in B they do lie in B'. Therefore, they form a set $Z = A \cap B'$ (see figure 4.1).

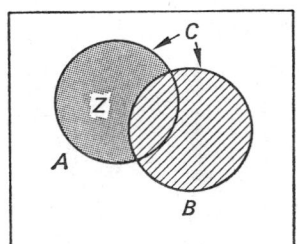

Fig. 4.1

By inspection, B and Z are exclusive and together they make up the whole of $C = A \cup B$.

Therefore, $P(A \cup B) = P(C) = P(B \cup Z)$
$\qquad\qquad\qquad\quad = P(B) + P(Z) \qquad\qquad$ Rule 3
$\qquad\qquad\qquad\quad = P(B) + P(A \cap B')$
$\qquad\qquad\qquad\quad = P(B) + P(A) - P(A \cap B). \quad$ see (3)

Therefore, $P(A \cup B) = P(A) + P(B) - P(A \cap B)$.

If A and B are exclusive, $A \cap B$ is empty and we reduce to Rule 3 itself:

$$P(A \cup B) = P(A) + P(B).$$

(5) If A and B are independent where $B \neq S$ (sample space)

$P(A \cap B) = P(A).P(B) \neq 0.$ definition

Therefore, $P(A \cap B') = P(A) - P(A \cap B)$ see (3)
$= P(A) - P(A).P(B)$
$= P(A)\{1 - P(B)\}$
$= P(A).P(B').$ see (1)

But $P(B') = 1 - P(B) > 0$ as $P(B) < 1$.
Therefore, $P(A).P(B') \neq 0$.
Therefore, A and B' are independent.

4.2 Problems and Answers

Probability problems can usually (and best) be dealt with in two separate stages, especially when they are based on equally likely situations. The first stage consists in identifying the event whose probability is being sought, and (where appropriate) counting over the set of 'successful' outcomes; the second consists of finding the probability itself, as often as not by the application of Rule 2.

PROBLEM 1

What is the probability that a bridge player finds all thirteen spades in his hand?

ANSWER

The number of possible hands is the number of ways of selecting 13 cards from 52, and this equals $\binom{52}{13}$, all equally likely (because the cards have been shuffled). The number of these consisting of all 13 spades is 1.

Therefore, the probability of all 13 spades $= 1/\binom{52}{13}$ Rule 2

$$= \frac{13!\,39!}{52!}.$$

4.2 THEORETICAL STATISTICS

PROBLEM 2

A player throws two dice; what is the probability that the two scores add to 9?

ANSWER

If the first die gives the number x and the second die gives the number y, the outcome of the experiment consists of the ordered pair of numbers (x, y). The number of possible pairs is 36, ranging from $(1, 1)$ to $(6, 6)$, and these are all equally likely. The pairs giving a total of 9 are $(3, 6)$ $(4, 5)$, $(5, 4)$, $(6, 3)$. Therefore probability of a 9 is $\frac{4}{36} = \frac{1}{9}$.

PROBLEM 3

Transistors are manufactured in bulk, and in a batch of N of them, a are defective. A random sample of n transistors is selected; what is the probability that the sample contains r defects? (It is given that $a \geqslant n \leqslant N - a$.)

ANSWER

The number of possible samples is $\binom{N}{n}$, all equally likely (because the sample is random). For a sample to contain r defects, r transistors must have been selected from the a defectives (and this can happen in $\binom{a}{r}$ ways) and $n - r$ from the $N - a$ non-defectives (and this can happen in $\binom{N-a}{n-r}$ ways). Therefore, the number of samples containing r defects is $\binom{a}{r} \cdot \binom{N-a}{n-r}$. Therefore, the probability of

$$r \text{ defects} = \binom{a}{r} \cdot \binom{N-a}{n-r} \bigg/ \binom{N}{n}$$

$$= \frac{a!(N-a)!n!(N-n)!}{r!(a-r)!(n-r)!(N-a-n+r)!N!}.$$

PROBLEM 4

Four people are dealt five cards each. The first player gets four hearts and one club. He discards the club, and takes in exchange the top card from the remaining 32. What is the probability he now has five hearts?

ANSWER

All that the first player knows is that the card he takes in exchange is not one of the five cards already in his hand; but it could be any of the other 47 cards. Admittedly the exchange card could not be one of the cards which happens to have been dealt to another player; but for that matter it could not be the card which happens to be second amongst the 32, or third, or fourth, etc. But as he does not know what has been dealt to the other players, or how the 32 cards are ordered, all this is irrelevant. The critical point is that all 47 unseen cards are in a random order, and consequently any one of them is equally likely to be in any position. In particular, all 47 cards are equally likely to be in the top position amongst the 32. But of these 47 cards, 9 are hearts.

Therefore, the probability that he finishes with five hearts equals the probability that the exchange card was a heart equals $\frac{9}{47}$.

PROBLEM 5

An urn contains x white balls and y black. The balls are extracted randomly one at a time until only one *colour* remains in the urn. What is the probability that the colour is white?

ANSWER

Suppose in a fit of enthusiasm the extractor continues until there is only one *ball* left in the urn. The colour of this last ball is obviously the same as the single colour remaining as set in the problem. Therefore, the probability that the single colour remaining is white equals the probability that the last ball in the

4.2 THEORETICAL STATISTICS

urn is white, which is $x/(x+y)$ because the last ball to be extracted is every bit as random as the first ball.

Notice here that we have seen what the required event was equivalent to before bringing in probabilities. It is as if we did the mathematics of events before doing the mathematics of probabilities. This often pays.

PROBLEM 6

If in a single trial the probability of a success is p, find the probability of precisely r successes in a sequence of n independent trials.

ANSWER

If the first trial leads to a failure (F)
If the second trial leads to a failure (F)
If the third trial leads to a success (S)
If the fourth trial leads to a failure (F)
we can represent the outcome as a whole by the sequence

$$\underbrace{F \quad F \quad S \quad F \quad \ldots\ldots}_{n \text{ terms}}$$

By independence, the probability of this sequence is

$$(1-p).(1-p).p.(1-p).\ldots = p^x.(1-p)^y,$$

where x is the number of S's, and y the number of F's.

Any two sequences containing x S's and y F's therefore have the same probability. We are interested in sequences containing r S's and consequently $(n-r)$ F's; each one of these has probability $p^r(1-p)^{n-r}$. But how many different sequences are there consisting of r S's and $(n-r)$ F's?

Any sequence is determined once it is settled which r of the n terms in the sequence are to be S's. Therefore, the number of different sequences is equal to the number of ways of selecting r things from n, i.e. to $\binom{n}{r}$. Each such sequence has probability

$p^r(1-p)^{n-r}$, therefore the probability of getting r S's and $(n-r)$ F's equals $\binom{n}{r}p^r(1-p)^{n-r}$.

PROBLEM 7

Three pennies are tossed; to find the probability they all come down the same. Suppose we argue:

(i) probability they are all heads $= \frac{1}{8}$.
probability they are all tails $= \frac{1}{8}$.
Therefore, probability they are all the same $= \frac{1}{8} + \frac{1}{8} = \frac{1}{4}$.

(ii) Of the three pennies, two must come down the same. The third comes down the same again, or different. Therefore, the probability all three are the same is determined by the third coin.
Therefore, the required probability $= \frac{1}{2}$.
How can both answers be correct?

ANSWER

They cannot. (i) is correct and (ii) is fallacious. Given a specific coin whose outcome is entirely unknown, the probability of a head is $\frac{1}{2}$. In our case it is uncertain which is the 'third' coin; it cannot always be identified until all three results are known, and by then it is too late to talk about probabilities.

(There is nothing like a good paradox for purging the mind!)

PROBLEM 8

I have two pennies in my pocket, one of them being two-headed. I draw one at random.

(i) What is the probability that it is two-headed?
(ii) I look at one side of it and see a head; what is the probability now that it is two-headed?

ANSWER

(i) $\frac{1}{2}$.
(ii) We can work this out using conditional probability. Let us, however, proceed from first principles. If the whole experi-

4.2 THEORETICAL STATISTICS

ment is performed many, many times, say N, then on roughly $N/2$ occasions I shall have the two-headed coin which must always show a head which ever way up I am holding it. On roughly $N/2$ occasions I shall have the proper penny, which half the time will have heads uppermost and half the time tails.

These frequencies are shown in the following table:

Coin	Frequency of heads	tails
two-headed	$\dfrac{N}{2}$	0
proper	$\dfrac{N}{4}$	$\dfrac{N}{4}$

We notice immediately that twice as many heads arise from the two-headed coin as from the proper coin; but we have a random head from the $\tfrac{3}{4}N$ heads. Therefore, the odds in favour of two-headedness is 2 to 1 (see footnote*).

Therefore probability of two-headedness is

$$\frac{2}{2+1} = \frac{2}{3}.$$

*If, in the long run, event A occurs r times as often as the complementary event A', we say that the odds in favour of A are r to 1. Out of N trials A will occur x times and A' y times, where $\dfrac{x}{y} = \dfrac{r}{1}$.

But $x + y = N$.

Solving these simultaneous equations:

$$x = \frac{Nr}{r+1}, \quad y = \frac{N}{r+1}.$$

Therefore, $P(A) = \dfrac{r}{r+1}$.

Conversely, if $P(A) = p$, the odds in favour of A are p to $(1-p)$.

5. Cumulative Distribution Functions

5.1 Random Variables

We have considered trials in which we can have any kind of outcome. Thus, drawing cards from a pack, an outcome might be the suit of the card, or it might be the value of the card. In this chapter, we are going to be interested in outcomes which are numbers. These numbers can arise naturally as with a die (where you get the outcomes 1, 2, 3, 4, 5, 6), or they might be imposed artificially on non-numerical data. Thus, in the football pools, the result of any match is a home win or an away win or a draw; but for the purposes of the pools, these outcomes are credited with the values 1, 2 and 3 (or some variants of these). We shall not bother here to distinguish between the natural and the artificial numbers; we are simply going to be interested in numbers however they arise as outcomes of experiments.

You will remember from your algebra that the letters $a, b, c, \ldots$ are conventionally used to represent fixed numbers, and letters x, y, z to represent variables. You may or may not have come across a rigorous definition of a variable; the odds are, however, that you became familiar with the nature and behaviour of variables simply by experience.

In general terms, the variable x can take any value in some specified range. Thus, if we have a function f with a domain R, the image of the function is normally expressed as $f(x)$. In this context, x is the variable; it can take any value from the set R. Just as x denotes an unknown or a variable in algebra, so X is used to denote the unknown or the variable in statistics. It is called a *random variable*. The random variable X can take any of the numerical outcomes of a trial just as the mathematical variable x can take any value in some

5.2 THEORETICAL STATISTICS

domain. What, then, is the difference? The difference is that with a statistical random variable, we are interested not only in the value it can take, but also in the probability with which it can take it. Thus, with a die, X can equal 1 (with probability $\frac{1}{6}$), or 2 (with probability $\frac{1}{6}$), and so on. If the die is biased in some way, the values 1 to 6 will still apply but the probabilities associated with them will differ.

Random variables can make notation very much simpler. For example, instead of spelling out at length 'the probability that a die takes the value 3 is equal to $\frac{1}{6}$', we can take X as being a random variable associated with the die, and then simply write $P(X = 3) = \frac{1}{6}$. This has introduced random variables and shown how they apply in a simple situation. They can, however, be used to represent the most general situation possible.

5.2 The Cumulative Distribution Function

If we have any random variable representing the outcomes of some trial, one of the basic questions we can ask is:

What is the value of $P(X \leqslant x)$?

If we were to know this value for all x, we would know about as much as we could about the situation.

The first thing we notice is that this gives us a mapping from x to $P(X \leqslant x)$. Indeed, this mapping is many–one, so it is a function (see footnote*). It is usual to denote this function by F. Thus,

$$P(X \leqslant x) = F(x) \quad (x \in \mathbb{R}).$$

F is called the *cumulative distribution function*, because it is concerned with all values of X from $-\infty$ up to x, as if the probabilities in question had been added together cumulatively. Let us, however, see how these cumulative distribution functions (c.d.f.'s for short) behave.

*Given a set A with elements a_i, and a set B with elements b_i, and a mapping from A to B, we say that the mapping is *many–one* if every element of A maps to a single element of B but where more than one element of A can map to the same element in B. Many–one mappings and *one–one* mappings are called *functions* as opposed to many–many or one–many mappings which are not functions.

CUMULATIVE DISTRIBUTION FUNCTIONS 5.3

First of all, $F(x)$ is a probability; therefore

$$0 \leqslant F(x) \leqslant 1 \text{ for all } x.\qquad \text{Rule 1}$$

Secondly if $x < x'$,

$X \leqslant x$ and $x < X \leqslant x'$ are exclusive events whose union is $X \leqslant x'$.

Therefore,
$$\begin{aligned}F(x') &= P(X \leqslant x') \\ &= P(X \leqslant x) + P(x < X \leqslant x') \qquad \text{Rule 3}\\ &\geqslant P(X \leqslant x) \\ &= F(x).\end{aligned}$$

Therefore, $F(x)$ increases (or stays constant) as x increases.

5.3 Examples of Cumulative Distribution Functions

Going back to our bicycle wheel (figure 5.1), it is exactly balanced if it is equally likely to stop in any position.

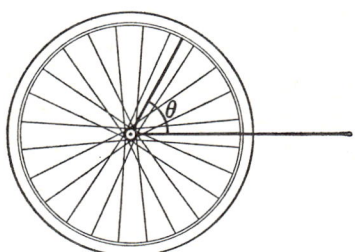

Fig. 5.1

In other words, θ can take any value from 0° to 360° and

$$F(x) = P(\theta \leqslant x)$$
$$= \frac{x}{360} \quad (0 \leqslant x < 360).$$

5.3 THEORETICAL STATISTICS

The graph of this function is shown in figure 5.2

The graph in this form is perfectly accurate. Thus, from the way in which the angle is measured, it is impossible for it to be negative.

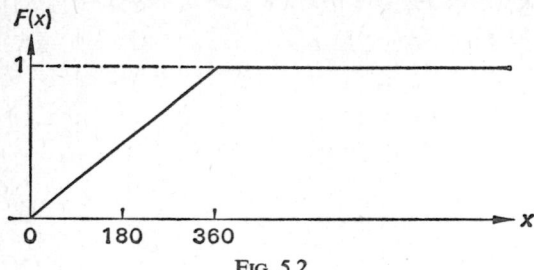

Fig. 5.2

Therefore, $F(x) = P(\theta \leqslant x) = 0$ if $x < 0$.

Equally, θ must be less than 360 (assuming that 360 itself would be recorded as 0).

Therefore, $F(x) = P(\theta \leqslant x) = 1$ if $x \geqslant 360$.

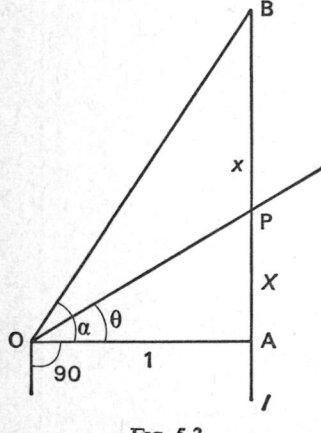

Fig. 5.3

Nevertheless, only the range (0, 360) is material, and therefore only this position need be plotted.

The fact that $F(x)$ increases with x (or stays constant) is apparent on sight. Also that $F(x)$ achieves its upper limit of 1 for all $x \geqslant 360$, and its lower limit of 0 for all $x \leqslant 0$.

$F(x)$ need not achieve its extreme values of 0 and 1. Consider, for example, a line rotating in a plane about a point which is unit distance from a fixed line l in the same plane (figure 5.3). The variable line meets l in a variable point P, and $X = AP$ is the random

CUMULATIVE DISTRIBUTION FUNCTIONS 5.3

variable we are interested in. Then X can take all values from $-\infty$ to $+\infty$.

Let angle AOP $= \theta$, and suppose that all values from -90 to $+90$ are equally likely for θ. Then

$$P(X \leq x) = P(\theta \leq a)$$

$$= \frac{90 + a}{180}, \quad \text{where } a \text{ will be negative for P below A,}$$

$$= \tfrac{1}{2} + \frac{a}{180}$$

$$= \tfrac{1}{2} + \frac{1}{180} \tan^{-1} x, \quad (-\infty < x < \infty).$$

Plotting the c.d.f. we get the graph shown in figure 5.4, indicating the manner in which $F(x)$ approaches its boundary values, yet without achieving them. The horizontal lines at heights 0 and 1 are

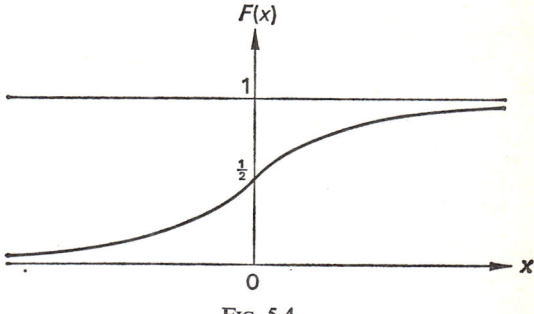

FIG. 5.4

asymptotes to the c.d.f., meaning that $F(x)$ tends to 0 (i.e. approaches 0 and in the long run stays as close to 0 as we please) as x tends to $-\infty$ and $F(x)$ tends to 1 as x tends to $+\infty$. The notation for this is

$$F(x) \rightsquigarrow 0 \text{ as } x \rightsquigarrow -\infty$$
$$\rightsquigarrow 1 \text{ as } x \rightsquigarrow +\infty.$$

5.3 THEORETICAL STATISTICS

This kind of property is true for all c.d.f.'s; that is

either (i) $F(x) = 1$ for all x sufficiently large and positive

or (ii) $F(x) \to 1$ as $x \to \infty$.

In the mathematical sense, (i) is really a sub-classification of (ii), though most non-mathematicians would not think of $F(x)$ as tending to 1 once it had arrived, for the word 'tending' conveys an impression of continuing travel.

Similarly, for all c.d.f.'s

either (i) $F(x) = 0$ for all x sufficiently large and negative

or (ii) $F(x) \to 0$ as $x \to -\infty$.

Finally, consider the throwing of a fair die. Here X can take only the values 1, 2, 3, 4, 5, 6. Nevertheless it is not nonsense to talk about $P(X \leq 2\cdot 4)$. X can satisfy this inequality, but only by taking the values 1 or 2.

Therefore, $P(X \leq 2\cdot 4) = P(X = 1 \text{ or } 2)$
$$= \tfrac{2}{6} = \tfrac{1}{3}.$$

X cannot be less than 1. But this does not lead to a contradiction; it merely implies that $P(X \leq x) = 0$ for all $x < 1$. Working out the probabilities for all x, we get the graph in figure 5.5.

The feature of this graph is that it is discontinuous; it jumps. Something not so obvious is precisely where the jumps come. Take $x < 1$; then however close x gets to 1,

$$F(x) = P(X \leq x) = 0,$$

but

$$F(1) = P(X \leq 1) = \tfrac{1}{6}.$$

In other words, there is a jump at $x = 1$; but by the time x has reached 1, the jump has already taken place. The jump lies on the left-hand side of the point $x = 1$. As x increases away from the value 1, $F(x)$ remains constant at the fixed value $\tfrac{1}{6}$. Again, as x approaches

CUMULATIVE DISTRIBUTION FUNCTIONS 5.4

2, $F(x)$ remains constant until 2 is reached when $F(x)$ jumps to $\frac{1}{3}$, etc. All the jumps are *on the left* of the jump points. This property is shared by all discontinuous c.d.f.'s.

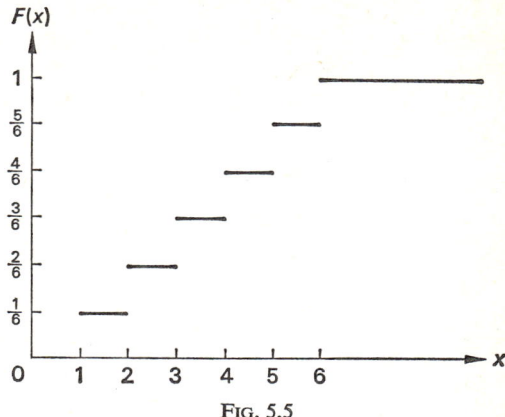

FIG. 5.5

It may seem unsymmetrical that all jumps should lie to the left of the jump points. But $F(x)$ itself is unsymmetrical as it is the probability $P(X \leqslant x)$. A function G given by

$$G(x) = P(X < x)$$

would have all jumps *on the right* of the jump points.

5.4 Summarising the Properties of C.D.F.'s

Through looking at particular c.d.f.'s, we have seen that they satisfy certain properties, namely:

(i) $0 \leqslant F(x) \leqslant 1 \quad (x \in R)$

$F(x) \to 0$ as $x \to -\infty$ including possibility that $F(x) = 0$.

$F(x) \to 1$ as $x \to +\infty$ including possibility that $F(x) = 1$.

(ii) $F(x)$ increases (or stays constant) as x increases.

5.4 THEORETICAL STATISTICS

(iii) If $F(x)$ has a jump at any point, the jump is always on the left of the point.

A natural question to ask is whether a mathematical function taken out of the blue—but satisfying the above three conditions—is a conceivable cumulative distribution function. The answer is yes. This is why c.d.f.'s are so important, because they associate random variables with mathematical functions, and vice versa. Every time you think of a random variable and the distribution of the random variable (i.e. the kind of values which the random variable can take and the probabilities with which it takes them) you think of the c.d.f. Once you know the c.d.f. of a random variable, there is nothing else to know about it, except possibly the actual values it takes on certain occasions. Also, every time you think of a function satisfying conditions (i), (ii) and (iii) above, you can think of a random variable having that function as its c.d.f. Thus, any theory of random variables is really the theory of a certain class of functions. In other words, statistics is a branch of the *theory of functions*. This might seem unduly restrictive, but it is not. There are some things a statistician does with his functions which many a mathematical analyst would not think of doing with his. Also, probability and statistics can bring in complex numbers, measure theory, vectors and matrices, difference equations, the theory of numbers including congruence arithmetic and Galois fields and even philosophy (brought in by inferential techniques).

After this little flurry, you may wonder how something which set out as probability and statistics involving the real world and practical experiments suddenly became an abstract part of mathematics. It happened when we wrote the equation

$$P(X \leqslant x) = F(x).$$

On the left-hand side is a probability associated with a random variable, and both these terms are associated with the external world. Probability is associated with relative frequency, and random variables with the outcomes of experiments. On the right-hand side, we have a mathematical function. The 'equals' sign in the middle is a kind of bridge between the two.

5.5 Bivariate Distributions

Sometimes data come in paired readings. Thus, if in a survey we select people, we might be interested in the heights and weights of all those selected. It would then be sensible to ask: 'If a person is selected randomly, what is the probability that his height is less than or equal to h and that his weight is less than or equal to w?' If H is a random variable standing for the height of a random person, and W is a random variable standing for the weight of the same random person, the probability we want is $P\{(H \leq h) \wedge (W \leq w)\}$. This is more usually denoted by:

$$P(H \leq h; W \leq w).$$

This expression can also be put in c.d.f. form as

$$P(H \leq h; W \leq w) = F(h, w).$$

We then say that F is a bivariate c.d.f. because it involves the two *variates* (or, as we now say, *random variables*) H and W. F satisfies conditions equivalent to (i), (ii) and (iii) above, but it is unnecessary for us to go into them here.

Taking the general bivariate c.d.f. given by

$$P(X \leq x; Y \leq y) = F(x, y),$$

it may be that the events
$$X \leq x$$
and
$$Y \leq y$$

are independent for all x and y. By definition, therefore,

$$\begin{aligned} F(x, y) &= P(X \leq x; Y \leq y) \\ &= P(X \leq x) . P(Y \leq y) \quad \text{by independence} \\ &= F_1(x) . F_2(y). \end{aligned}$$

In other words, the variables x and y separate out. In this situation, we say that the random variables X and Y are independent.

Let us look at a consequence of this. If (X, Y) from a bivariate distribution is such that $x < X \leqslant x'$, how does this affect the probability that $y < Y \leqslant y'$?

Now

$P(x < X \leqslant x') \cdot P(y < Y \leqslant y'/x < X \leqslant x')$
$= P(x < X \leqslant x'; y < Y \leqslant y')$ Rule 4
$= P(x < X \leqslant x') \cdot P(y < Y \leqslant y')$.   follows from independence

Cancelling by $P(x < X \leqslant x')$,   (assuming non-zero)

$P(y < Y \leqslant y'/x < X \leqslant x') = P(y < Y \leqslant y'),$

or the conditional probability on Y is equal to the unconditional. Thus a knowledge of X tells us nothing about Y.

5.6 Multivariate Distributions

The bivariate distribution involving two random variables extends naturally into the multivariate distribution involving (say) k random variables. Starting with X, Y, Z, we run out of letters, so we have to change our notation to:

$$P(X_1 \leqslant x_1; X_2 \leqslant x_2; \ldots X_k \leqslant x_k) = F(x_1, x_2, \ldots x_k).$$

If the random variables are completely independent, then

$$\begin{aligned} F(x_1, x_2, \ldots x_k) &= P(X_1 \leqslant x_1; X_2 \leqslant x_2; \ldots X_k \leqslant x_k) \\ &= P(X_1 \leqslant x_1) \cdot P(X_2 \leqslant x_2) \ldots \\ &\qquad P(X_k \leqslant x_k) \quad \text{by independence} \\ &= F_1(x_1) \cdot F_2(x_2) \ldots F_k(x_k) \end{aligned}$$

where $F_1(x_1)$ is the c.d.f. of X_1 separately, and so on. Conversely, if $F(x_1, x_2, \ldots x_k) = F_1(x_1) \cdot F_2(x_2) \ldots F_k(x_k)$, then the random variables $X_1, X_2, \ldots X_k$ are completely independent.

6. Discrete Distributions

If a random variable can take only certain discrete values (e.g. if it comes from a die rather than from a bicycle wheel), the cumulative distribution function is rather a clumsy way of representing the situation. All we need to know about X are the values $a_0, a_1, a_2, \ldots$ it can take, and the probabilities $p_0, p_1, p_2, \ldots$ with which it takes them. We can express all this mathematically in the form

$$P(X = a_r) = p_r \qquad r = 0, 1, 2, \ldots.$$

Having a simpler form to work with, we can now easily cope with one of the fundamental notions in statistics.

6.1 Expectations

If X is a random variable standing for the number on a die when it is thrown, X takes values from 1 to 6 with certain frequencies; but, what is the average value of X? Relying on familiar ideas, we could take a large number N of trials, add together all the values occurring, and divide by N. This is all right up to a point, but we do not want to rely on the extraneous N. We want the average over the whole distribution; yet we cannot put $N = \infty$, for this makes a nonsense of the formula. As usual when meeting problems imposed by the infinite, we get out of trouble by proceeding to the limit.

If in N trials there are m_1 1's
m_2 2's
.
.
.
m_6 6's

6.1 THEORETICAL STATISTICS

then the total score $= 1.m_1 + 2.m_2 + \ldots + 6.m_6$.

Therefore, the average score $= 1.\dfrac{m_1}{N} + 2.\dfrac{m_2}{N} + \ldots + 6.\dfrac{m_6}{N}$.

Now m_1/N is the relative frequency of 1's, and, as N tends to infinity, we have always supposed that relative frequency tends to the probability of the event. In other words, for a fair die,

$$\frac{m_1}{N} \text{ tends to } \tfrac{1}{6}.$$

Similarly, $\dfrac{m_2}{N}$ tends to $\tfrac{1}{6}$, and so on.

We would therefore expect the average score to tend to

$$1.\tfrac{1}{6} + 2.\tfrac{1}{6} + \ldots + 6.\tfrac{1}{6}$$
$$= 3\cdot 5 \text{ as } N \to \infty.$$

Now this relies on suppositions which we can never get to infinity to check. Secondly, what we have worked out is not strictly an average itself, but what we expect the average to be as $N \to \infty$. To curtail what in any case would only be a futile argument, we go straight to the value

$$1.\tfrac{1}{6} + 2.\tfrac{1}{6} + \ldots + 6.\tfrac{1}{6}$$

and define it to be the *expectation of X*.

If the die were biased so that

$$P(X = r) = p_r \quad r = 1, 2, \ldots 6$$

the corresponding value is

$$1.p_1 + 2.p_2 + \ldots 6.p_6.$$

For the general distribution

$$P(X = a_r) = p_r$$

we would have the *expectation of X*, $E(X) = \sum_r a_r p_r$

DISCRETE DISTRIBUTIONS 6.2

If there is only a finite number of a's, $\sum_r a_r p_r$ is the *weighted arithmetic mean* of the a's, the weights being the probabilities p_r.

Sometimes we are interested not so much in X itself as in some image of X. Thus, if ball bearings were being produced, and X was the radius of a random one, then to get at the average volume we would think of $E(\frac{4}{3}\pi X^3)$. In general, if h was any function, we could be interested in $E\{h(X)\}$.

From its definition, expectations can be seen to satisfy many properties which are very useful mathematically. Thus

(i) $E(1) = \sum_r 1 \cdot p_r = \sum_r p_r = 1$, as the total probability is 1.

(ii) If λ is any constant
$$E(\lambda) = \sum_r \lambda p_r = \lambda \sum_r p_r = \lambda.$$

(iii) $E\{\lambda h(X)\} = \sum_r \lambda h(a_r) p_r$
$$= \lambda \sum_r h(a_r) p_r$$
$$= \lambda E\{h(X)\}.$$

(iv) $E\{\sum_i h_i(X)\} = \sum_r \{h_1(a_r) + h_2(a_r) + \ldots\} p_r$
$$= \sum_r h_1(a_r) p_r + \sum_r h_2(a_r) p_r + \ldots$$
$$= E\{h_1(X)\} + E\{h_2(X)\} + \ldots$$
$$= \sum_i E\{h_i(X)\}.$$

Thus we see that expectations are additive.

6.2 Moments

One seldom travels far in mathematics without meeting powers of variables. Thus polynomials are always cropping up, and these are simply sums of powers of x with coefficients thrown in. As soon as we meet $\sin x$ we are out to show and to use the fact that

$$\sin x = x - \frac{x^3}{3!} + \frac{x^5}{5!} - \ldots.$$

Statistics is no exception; only here it is not so much X^r which crops

6.2 THEORETICAL STATISTICS

up as $E(X^r)$. We therefore give these values names. They are called *moments* of the distribution of X, and are denoted by μ'; thus

$$\mu'_r = E(X^r) = r\text{th moment}.$$

(i) $\mu'_0 = E(X^0) = E(1) = 1$.

(ii) $\mu'_1 = E(X)$, which is also called the *mean* of the distribution of X. It is often denoted simply by μ.

(iii) Although the mean μ has been defined for a distribution, and represents a very simple idea, it would be a mistake to suppose that it always existed. Consider, for example, the distribution of

$$P(X = r+1) = \frac{1}{(r+1)(r+2)} \quad r = 0, 1, 2, \ldots .$$

This is a perfectly genuine distribution; all the probabilities are positive, and their sum is

$$\frac{1}{1.2} + \frac{1}{2.3} + \ldots = 1.$$

[This result can be seen by writing

$$\frac{1}{1.2} + \frac{1}{2.3} + \frac{1}{3.4} + \ldots$$

$$= (\tfrac{1}{1} - \tfrac{1}{2}) + (\tfrac{1}{2} - \tfrac{1}{3}) + (\tfrac{1}{3} - \tfrac{1}{4}) + \ldots$$

$$= 1].$$

But the mean is

$$E(X) = \sum_{r=0}^{\infty} (r+1) \frac{1}{(r+1)(r+2)}$$

$$= \sum \frac{1}{r+2}$$

$$= \tfrac{1}{2} + \tfrac{1}{3} + \tfrac{1}{4} + \tfrac{1}{5} + \ldots$$

which is divergent, having no finite sum.

[This result can be seen by writing

$$\tfrac{1}{2} + (\tfrac{1}{3} + \tfrac{1}{4}) + (\tfrac{1}{5} + \tfrac{1}{6} + \tfrac{1}{7} + \tfrac{1}{8}) + \ldots$$
$$\triangleright \tfrac{1}{2} + (\tfrac{1}{4} + \tfrac{1}{4}) + (\tfrac{1}{8} + \tfrac{1}{8} + \tfrac{1}{8} + \tfrac{1}{8}) + \ldots$$
$$= \tfrac{1}{2} + \tfrac{2}{4} + \tfrac{4}{8} + \ldots$$
$$= \tfrac{1}{2} + \tfrac{1}{2} + \tfrac{1}{2} + \ldots].$$

If the mean does not always exist, you must not be surprised if higher moments of distributions do not always exist.

6.3 Moments about the Mean

Although the moments of a distribution tell us something about the distribution, it is difficult at this stage to say what they tell us. Alternatively, it is difficult to see the relevance of what they tell us. So if they can be improved in some way, so much the better. One trouble with them is that they change if the origin changes. If you are measuring the temperature of some substance, and get values

$$25° \quad 26° \quad 24° \quad 24° \quad 28° \quad \ldots,$$

these are by no means the same as the values

$$75° \quad 76° \quad 74° \quad 74° \quad 78° \quad \ldots,$$

simply because it may be material that a higher temperature is involved. But if we were undecided whether to express the temperature in Celsius (as above) or in Kelvin, and so were oscillating between the series

$$25 \quad 26 \quad 24 \quad 24 \quad 28 \quad \ldots,$$

and

$$298 \quad 299 \quad 297 \quad 297 \quad 301 \quad \ldots,$$

it would be a pity if the experimental results, which were constant in themselves, appeared to change merely because of a shift in the origin. It is important to have characteristics of a distribution which are independent of the origin selected. The 'moments' would be

6.3 THEORETICAL STATISTICS

independent in this way if they were taken about the mean value of the data instead of about zero.

These remarks made about experimental results apply equally to theoretical distributions as a whole. In this case, the moments can be transformed so as to be independent of the origin. We do this by taking *moments about the mean*, denoting them by μ_r. Thus

$$\mu_r = E(X - \mu)^r.$$

It should be noticed that moments as defined originally were in effect moments about the origin, and their symbol μ'_r carries a prime; moments about the mean are symbolised by μ_r which does not carry the prime.

As before, let us look at some special cases.

(i) $\mu_0 = E(X - \mu)^0 = E(1) = 1$

(ii) $\mu_1 = E(X - \mu) = E(X) - \mu = 0$

(iii) $\mu_2 = E(X - \mu)^2.$

We call μ_2 the *variance* of the distribution. Also $\sigma = +\sqrt{\mu_2}$ is called the *standard deviation*.

(iv) If the distribution has zero mean,
$$\mu_r = E(X - 0)^r = E(X^r) = \mu'_r.$$

The next obvious question to ask is how the two kinds of moments are related. Below, we obtain the relationship for $r = 2$:

$$\begin{aligned}
\mu_2 &= E(X - \mu)^2 \\
&= E(X^2 - 2\mu X + \mu^2) \\
&= E(X^2) - E(2\mu X) + E(\mu^2) \quad \text{by additive rule} \\
&\qquad\qquad\qquad\qquad\qquad\qquad\qquad \text{for expectations} \\
&= E(X^2) - 2\mu E(X) + E(\mu^2) \\
&= E(X^2) - 2\mu . \mu + \mu^2 \\
&= E(X^2) - \mu^2 \\
&= \mu'_2 - \mu^2.
\end{aligned}$$

Anyone interested in further cases can obtain them for himself.

We set out with the intention of providing characteristic values

DISCRETE DISTRIBUTIONS 6.4

which were independent of the origin selected. Let us verify that this has been achieved.

If X is a random variable and Y is the same random variable when referred to a different origin, then $Y = X + h$.
(In our temperature example, if X were the value in Celsius and Y in Kelvin, then $h = 273$.)

If
$$E(X) = \mu$$
then
$$E(Y) = E(X + h)$$
$$= E(X) + h$$
$$= \mu + h.$$

Therefore, the rth moment of Y about its mean
$$= E\{Y - (\mu + h)\}^r$$
$$= E(X + h - \mu - h)^r$$
$$= E(X - \mu)^r$$
$$= r\text{th moment of } X \text{ about its mean.}$$

6.4 Transformation of Random Variables

The work above is an example of the *transformation* of a random variable. It shows what happens to moments about the mean when we go from X to $Y = X + h$. Let us see what happens when we go from X to $Y = \lambda X$.

$$\text{Mean of } (Y) = E(Y)$$
$$= E(\lambda X)$$
$$= \lambda E(X)$$
$$= \lambda \mu.$$

The rth moment of Y about its mean
$$= E\{Y - E(Y)\}^r$$
$$= E(\lambda X - \lambda \mu)^r$$
$$= \lambda^r E(X - \mu)^r$$
$$= \lambda^r \times r\text{th moment of } X \text{ about its mean.}$$

6.5 THEORETICAL STATISTICS

This is of immediate practical importance. For if X is a measurement in centimetres, and Y the corresponding measurement in millimetres

$$Y = 10X.$$

Therefore, the variance of $(Y) = 10^2 \times$ variance of (X).

Hence, if you choose to work in millimetres so as to avoid a decimal point, this is quite all right; you can find the variance of Y, but then have to divide by 100 to obtain the variance of X.

We have covered change of origin and also change of scale. Let us run the two together, as in the following example.

If X is a random variable with mean μ and standard deviation σ, then $X - \mu$ has mean 0 and standard deviation σ (because the variance is unaffected by change of origin).

Therefore, $\dfrac{X - \mu}{\sigma}$ has mean 0 and standard deviation 1

(because the mean is $\dfrac{1}{\sigma} \times$ mean of $(X - \mu) = 0$ and variance of $\dfrac{X - \mu}{\sigma}$ is $\dfrac{1}{\sigma^2} \times$ variance of $(X - \mu) = \dfrac{1}{\sigma^2} \times \sigma^2 = 1$).

6.5 More General Transformation

Given a random variable X with distribution

$$P(X = a_r) = p_r \qquad r = 0, 1, 2, \ldots$$

the question can arise as to the distribution of

$$Y = h(X), \text{ where } h \text{ is some function.}$$

We have already had particular cases of this, namely

$$Y = \frac{x - \mu}{\sigma} \quad \text{when } h \text{ is linear}$$

and

$$Y = \tfrac{4}{3}\pi X^3 \quad \text{when } h \text{ is cubic.}$$

In general, of course, h need not be algebraic.

Now $$P(X = a_r) = p_r,$$
and every time $$X = a_r, \ Y = h(a_r)$$
$$= b_r, \text{ say}$$
Therefore, $$P(Y = b_r) = P(X = a_r) = p_r.$$

This is the most direct approach, but it requires correct interpretation. Thus, if we have

$$P(X = -1) = \tfrac{1}{3}$$
$$P(X = 0) = \tfrac{1}{3}$$
$$P(X = 1) = \tfrac{1}{3}$$
$$Y = X^2$$

then
$$P(Y = 0) = \tfrac{1}{3}$$
$$P(Y = 1) = \tfrac{1}{3} + \tfrac{1}{3} = \tfrac{2}{3}$$

because the value 1 crops up twice for Y.

Luckily, we do not always have to work out the distribution of Y. We saw this in the simple case of a linear transformation, for if

$$Y = aX + \beta$$

and all we are interested in is the mean and variance of Y, we have already observed that

$$E(Y) = a\mu$$
$$\text{var}(Y) = a^2\sigma^2,$$

where μ and σ^2 are the mean and variance of X.

6.6 Inequalities Involving Moments of a Distribution

(i) Given the distribution

$$P(X = a_r) = p_r \quad r = 0, 1, 2, \ldots$$

in which

$a_r \geq 0$ for all r
$a_r > 0$ for some r
t is any positive number,
the mean will be some value $\mu > 0$.

6.6 THEORETICAL STATISTICS

Let $\sum_r'$ denote summation over all values of r (if any) for which $a_r \geqslant \mu t$; then

$$\mu = \sum_r a_r p_r \qquad \text{by definition}$$
$$\geqslant \sum_r' a_r p_r \qquad \text{as } a_r \geqslant 0$$
$$\geqslant \sum_r' \mu t p_r$$
$$= \mu t \sum_r' p_r$$
$$= \mu t P(X \geqslant \mu t)$$

Therefore, $\quad P(X \geqslant \mu t) \leqslant \dfrac{1}{t}$.

(ii) If a random variable X has mean μ and variance $\sigma^2 > 0$, and t is any positive number, let $Y = (X - \mu)^2$. Then Y never takes negative values, and

$$E(Y) = E(X - \mu)^2$$
$$= \sigma^2 > 0.$$

Therefore,
$$P(\mu - t\sigma < X < \mu + t\sigma)$$
$$= P(-t\sigma < X - \mu < t\sigma)$$
$$= P\{(X - \mu)^2 < t^2\sigma^2\}$$
$$= P(Y < t^2\sigma^2)$$
$$= 1 - P(Y \geqslant t^2\sigma^2)$$
$$= 1 - P\{Y \geqslant t^2 . E(Y)\}$$
$$\geqslant 1 - \frac{1}{t^2} \text{ by (i)}.$$

The complementary form of this is:

$$P\{|X - \mu| \geqslant t\sigma\} \leqslant \frac{1}{t^2}.$$

This is known as *Tchebycheff's Inequality* (after the Russian mathematician, P. L. Tchebycheff, 1821–94), and it is one of the remarkable results of elementary probability theory. It says that, whatever the distribution, a random variable has probability $1 - 1/t^2$ or more of lying within distance $t\sigma$ of its mean. Put the

DISCRETE DISTRIBUTIONS 6.7

other way round, the probability that a random variable X deviates from its mean by $t\sigma$ or more is less than or equal to $1/t^2$. Taking $t = 2$, and a distribution having zero mean and unit variance, the probability that X lies on or outside $+2$ is less than or equal to $\frac{1}{4}$. This should help to bring out something of the significance of both means and variances.

6.7 Moment Generating Functions

We have already met the probability terms

$$p_r = \binom{n}{r} p^r (1-p)^{n-r}.$$

We now note that if we expand the expression $\{(1-p) + pt\}^n$ in powers of t, we get:

$$\{(1-p) + pt\}^n = (1-p)^n + \binom{n}{1} p(1-p)^{n-1} t +$$

$$+ \binom{n}{2} p^2 (1-p)^{n-2} t^2 + \ldots + p^n t^n \text{ from the binomial theorem}$$

$$= p_0 + p_1 t + p_2 t + \ldots + p_n t^n.$$

Thus p_r is the coefficient of t^r. Hence the expression $\{(1-p) + pt\}^n$ *generates* our probabilities; it can therefore be called a *probability generating function*. We ask ourselves here, however, whether there is such a thing as a moment generating function; that is, whether a function ϕ exists such that the coefficients of θ in the expansion of $\phi(\theta)$ are the moments μ'_r of our distribution. Actually, we shall find it convenient to modify this question slightly.

Taking the general distribution

$$P(X = a_r) = p_r \quad r = 0, 1, 2, \ldots$$

consider the rectangular array of numbers,

55

6.7 THEORETICAL STATISTICS

$$p_0 \quad \frac{\theta a_0}{1!}p_0 \quad \frac{(\theta a_0)^2}{2!}p_0 \quad \frac{(\theta a_0)^3}{3!}p_0 \quad \ldots$$

$$p_1 \quad \frac{\theta a_1}{1!}p_1 \quad \frac{(\theta a_1)^2}{2!}p_1 \quad \frac{(\theta a_1)^3}{3!}p_1 \quad \ldots$$

$$p_2 \quad \frac{\theta a_2}{1!}p_2 \quad \frac{(\theta a_2)^2}{2!}p_2 \quad \frac{(\theta a_2)^3}{3!}p_2 \quad \ldots$$

$$\cdot \quad \cdot \quad \cdot \quad \cdot$$
$$\cdot \quad \cdot \quad \cdot \quad \cdot$$
$$\cdot \quad \cdot \quad \cdot \quad \cdot$$

If we want to add them all up, we can obtain the row totals and add, or obtain the column totals and add. In either case, we get the same grand total (this can be established mathematically for the kind of value which occurs in statistics).

A typical row total is

$$R_r = p_r + \frac{\theta a_r}{1!}p_r + \frac{(\theta a_r)^2}{2!}p_r + \frac{(\theta a_r)^3}{3!}p_r + \ldots$$

$$= p_r\{1 + u + \frac{u^2}{2!} + \frac{u^3}{3!} + \ldots\}, \text{ where } u = \theta a_r$$

$$= p_r e^u = p_r e^{\theta a_r}.$$

Therefore, grand total $= \sum_r R_r = \sum_r e^{\theta a_r} p_r$

$$= E(e^{\theta X}).$$

A typical column total is

$$C_s = \frac{(\theta a_0)^s}{s!}p_0 + \frac{(\theta a_1)^s}{s!}p_1 + \frac{(\theta a_2)^s}{s!}p_2 + \ldots$$

$$= \frac{\theta^s}{s!}\{a_0{}^s p_0 + a_1{}^s p_1 + a_2{}^s p_2 + \ldots\}$$

$$= \frac{\theta^s}{s!}\sum_r a_r{}^s p_r = \frac{\theta^s}{s!}E(X^s) \quad = \frac{\theta^s}{s!}\mu'_s.$$

Therefore, grand total $= \sum_s C_s = \sum_s \mu'_s \frac{\theta^s}{s!}.$

But these two grand totals are equal.

Therefore, $E(e^{\theta X}) = \sum_s \mu'_s \frac{\theta^s}{s!}$

$$= 1 + \mu'_1 \theta + \mu'_2 \frac{\theta^2}{2!} + \mu'_3 \frac{\theta^3}{3!} + \ldots.$$

Hence, we have obtained an expression which, when expanded in terms of the variable θ, has the moments as coefficients of $\theta^s/s!$. This is important primarily because of its convenience.

(a) If we could find a moment generating function of a distribution, then at one swoop we would have all the moments.
(b) It is usually the case that the moments of a distribution uniquely determine that distribution. Thus if we have an unknown distribution, but can show that its moments are the same as those for some known distribution, then we can identify the unknown distribution. But, rather than finding all the moments, it would be far quicker merely to identify the two moment generating functions; for then all the moments must equate.
(c) If a distribution does not have all its moments (you will recall that we have already seen a distribution which did not even have a first moment), then it will not have a generating function. In this case other methods have to be used.

7. Particular Discrete Distributions

7.1 Die Distribution

If X is a random variable representing the numbers coming up on a fair die, we have already accepted that

$$P(X = r) = \tfrac{1}{6} \quad r = 1, 2, \ldots 6.$$

But this is a statement of a distribution. For want of a better name, we shall call it the *die distribution*. The moments may be found as follows:

(i) Mean $= E(X)$

$$= \sum_{r=1}^{6} r \times \tfrac{1}{6}$$

$$= \tfrac{1}{6}(1 + 2 + 3 + 4 + 5 + 6)$$

$$= 3 \cdot 5.$$

(ii) $\mu'_2 = E(X^2)$

$$= \sum_{r=1}^{6} r^2 \times \tfrac{1}{6}$$

$$= \tfrac{1}{6}(1 + 4 + 9 + 16 + 25 + 36)$$

$$= \tfrac{91}{6}.$$

(iii) Variance $= \mu_2 = \mu'_2 - \mu^2$

$$= \tfrac{91}{6} - \tfrac{49}{4}$$

$$= \tfrac{182 - 147}{12}$$

$$= \tfrac{35}{12}.$$

In the same manner, it is possible to get the moments of the more general distribution

$$P(X = r) = \frac{1}{n} \qquad r = 1, 2, \ldots n.$$

7.2 Binomial Distribution

In Chapter 4 (Problem 6), we found the probability of getting r successes out of n trials, when the probability of success in a single trial was p. If the number of successes is represented by the random variable X, we found in effect that

$$P(X = r) = \binom{n}{r} p^r (1-p)^{n-r} \qquad r = 0, 1, 2, \ldots n.$$

This is in the form of a distribution. For reasons which are given below, it is called the *binomial distribution*, and X is then called a *binomial random variable*; n and p are called *parameters* of the distribution.

For any distribution, the probabilities must sum to 1. Let us confirm that this occurs here.

$$\text{Sum of probabilities} = \sum_{r=0}^{n} \binom{n}{r} p^r (1-p)^{n-r}$$

$$= \{(1-p) + p\}^n \quad \text{by the binomial theorem}$$

$$= 1^n = 1.$$

Thus the distribution is intimately associated with the binomial theorem, and so borrows its name.

Finding the moments is more a question of mathematical technique than of any new basic concept, so we will not give the working here. Nevertheless, they are worth quoting, and come out to be:

$$E(X) = np$$

$$\text{Variance } (X) = np(1-p).$$

These results will come in useful in the next chapter when we look at a law of large numbers.

7.3 THEORETICAL STATISTICS

7.3 Poisson Distribution

The distribution given by

$$P(X = r) = e^{-m} \frac{m^r}{r!} \quad r = 0, 1, 2, \ldots$$

is named after the French mathematician, S. D. Poisson (1781–1840). The total probability is clearly unity (as it should be) for

$$\sum_{r=0}^{\infty} e^{-m} \frac{m^r}{r!} = e^{-m}\left(1 + m + \frac{m^2}{2!} + \frac{m^3}{3!} + \cdots\right)$$
$$= e^{-m} \cdot e^m$$
$$= 1.$$

The distribution is important because in certain cases it is a good approximation to the binomial distribution. More precisely, if a binomial distribution is such that

n is pretty large,

p is pretty small,

then it is approximately the same as the Poisson distribution having parameter $m = np$; thus

$$P(X = r) \text{ is approximately equal to } e^{-np} \frac{(np)^r}{r!}.$$

You may still wonder why the Poisson distribution matters. If a distribution is accurately binomial and only approximately Poisson, why bother with the Poisson? The reasons are:

(i) If one binomial distribution had parameters n_1, p_1, and another n_2, p_2, they would be very similar if

both n's were pretty large

both p's were pretty small

$n_1 p_1 = n_2 p_2.$

PARTICULAR DISCRETE DISTRIBUTIONS 7.3

This fact could be material for you, but without expressing each binomial distribution in terms of its Poisson approximation, you would not realise the fact.

(ii) The binomial distribution has two parameters n and p, while the Poisson distribution has only one, m. The Poisson distribution is therefore simpler, and you would prefer to use it, just as you would rather fit a straight line to points on a graph than a curve if you reasonably could.

(iii) The Poisson distribution can arise in practice as an approximation to the binomial. Thus if a Geiger counter is placed in a radioactive field, and in any one-tenth of a second there is a probability of $\frac{1}{100}$ that a particle operates the counter, the random variable representing the number of particles counted in one minute is clearly binomial with

$$n = 60 \times 10 = 600 = \text{large}$$

$$p = \frac{1}{100} = \text{small}.$$

Therefore the distribution is approximately Poisson with parameter $m = np = 6$.

Now to begin with you will not know the value of p. You can choose the time interval of $\frac{1}{10}$ second for yourself; but this is an embarrassment if anything, for it appears to introduce an element of arbitrariness. But if you once know m, you can immediately write down the distribution for the number of particles per minute. You would want to know m in any case, for it is the mean of the Poisson distribution, and so is equal to the expected number of particles per minute. This is just the way you would specify the strength of the radioactive field; you would refer to the average number of particles crossing some boundary in unit time. Thus, from a knowledge of (or after estimating) the strength of the radioactive field, you can immediately write down the probability of getting any specified number of particles in any minute. This is surely a convenient fact.

In the demonstration of (iii) above, we have spoken of a particle arriving or not arriving in each $\frac{1}{10}$ second. By implication at least,

7.3 THEORETICAL STATISTICS

we have rejected the idea of two or more arriving in the same sub-interval. This is reasonable on the face of it, for if the probability of one particle is as small as $\frac{1}{100}$, the probability of two or more must be negligible. If, for other figures, this probability is not negligible, then in those cases our conclusions do not apply. But we do not need to worry about it. If we are in serious doubt about the issue, all we have to do is to experiment over a number of different minutes and see whether the numbers of particles counted do fit a Poisson distribution.

The Poisson distribution can arise in circumstances which superficially look very different. Thus it can represent not the number of nuclear particles per minute but the number of telephone calls initiated at an exchange per minute. This indeed is how Post Office engineers work out how many cables and pieces of equipment are required. Knowing the average number of calls per minute, they can work out the probability of overloading the capacity of the exchange.

We have made rather a feature of the Poisson distribution; but not because it is the central distribution in statistics—in fact, it is not. It is, however, less familiar than some other distributions; and it does provide a good example of how statisticians operate, of how they use approximation methods, and on what basis they would prefer one treatment to another.

8. A Law of Large Numbers

There is more than one law of large numbers, and probably many different versions of each at that. We shall look at just one version of one law which can be stated as follows:

- If, in a single trial, the probability of an event is p, and in a run of n independent trials the event occurs a total of X times, then X/n tends to approach p as n tends to infinity.

8.1 Remarks

For us, probability is linked with the idea of the limit of a relative frequency, and the law is merely a re-expression of this idea. Any proof of the law is only proving what we have always assumed to be the case; proof is therefore superfluous and circular. On the other hand, there is a form of proof which tells us a bit more about the situation than we knew previously. But first, let us examine the wording of the law more closely.

The statement is that 'X/n tends to approach p as n tends to infinity'. It does not say 'X/n tends to p' for this would be false. However large n may be, it is never certain that X/n lies within some interval $(p - \varepsilon, p + \varepsilon)$. If this is not certain, how can we water things down to get a relevant statement which is true? By saying (if

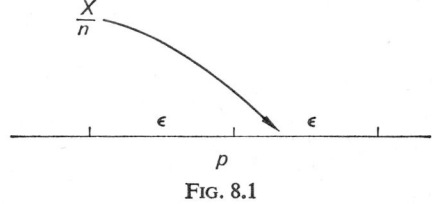

FIG. 8.1

8.1 THEORETICAL STATISTICS

we can) 'it is probable that X/n lies within $(p - \varepsilon, p + \varepsilon)$. See figure 8.1.

If X represents the total number of occurrences of some event in n independent trials, then X is a binomial random variable having

$$\text{mean} \quad np$$
$$\text{variance} \quad np(1-p).$$

Let Y be a transformation of X given by

$$Y = \frac{X}{n},$$

then

$$E(Y) = E\left(\frac{X}{n}\right) = \frac{np}{n} = p$$

$$\text{var}(Y) = \text{var}\left(\frac{X}{n}\right)$$

$$= \frac{1}{n^2} \text{var}(X)$$

$$= \frac{np(1-p)}{n^2}$$

$$= \frac{p(1-p)}{n}.$$

Therefore,

$$P\left\{\left|\frac{X}{n} - p\right| \geq t\right\} = P\{|Y - p| \geq t\}$$

$$= P\left\{|Y - p| \geq t\sqrt{\frac{n}{p(1-p)}} \cdot \sqrt{\frac{p(1-p)}{n}}\right\}$$

$$= P\left\{|Y - p| \geq u\sqrt{\frac{p(1-p)}{n}}\right\}$$

A LAW OF LARGE NUMBERS 8.2

$$\left[\text{where } u = t\sqrt{\frac{n}{p(1-p)}}\right]$$

$$\leqslant \frac{1}{u^2} \text{ by Tchebycheff}$$

$$= \frac{p(1-p)}{nt^2}$$

$\rightarrow 0$ as $n \rightarrow \infty$ for fixed p, t.

Therefore,

$$P\left\{\left|\frac{X}{n} - p\right| < t\right\} = 1 - P\left\{\left|\frac{X}{n} - p\right| \geqslant t\right\}$$

$\rightarrow 1$ as $n \rightarrow \infty$.

While, therefore, it is not true that $X/n \rightarrow p$, it is true that the probability of X/n lying as close as we please to p does tend to 1. (It is this probability statement which is the 'bit more' we did not know previously.) Against a probability background of uncertainties, this is the best we can do; but if you think about it, it is a pretty good 'best'.

The other feature of the situation is the use of Tchebycheff's inequality. The inequality looks weak. According to Tchebycheff, the probability of a random variable lying on or outside a distance of 2σ from the mean is less than or equal to ·25, whereas for one particular distribution it is as low as ·05. Yet because we have an n which tends to infinity, Tchebycheff is able to make us as confident as we please (95%?, 99%?, 99·9%?) that X/n is as near to p as we please (·1?, ·01?, ·001?) simply by taking n sufficiently large.

8.2 Stochastic Limits

In the ordinary mathematical sense of the word, p is not the limit of X/n; we therefore have to give it a special name. We call p the *stochastic limit*; also we say that X/n *tends to p stochastically*.

8.2 THEORETICAL STATISTICS

(*Stochastic* comes from a Greek word meaning 'aim' or 'guess'.) There is a whole theory of stochastic processes concerned with certain kinds of random variables possessing stochastic limits. Stochastic limits are also relevant to estimation theory; but that must be a topic for another occasion.

9. Discrete Bivariate Distributions

Just as a discrete distribution given by a cumulative distribution function F can be more conveniently expressed in the form

$$P(X = a_r) = p_r,$$

so bivariate distributions given by a c.d.f. can be more conveniently expressed in the form

$$P(X = a_r; Y = b_s) = p_{r,s}.$$

If the random variables X and Y are independent, then by definition

$$P(X \leqslant a_r; Y \leqslant b_s) = P(X \leqslant a_r) . P(Y \leqslant b_s) \quad \text{(see Chapter 5)}.$$

In this case, you will not be surprised to learn that

$$P(X = a_r; Y = b_s) = P(X = a_r) . P(Y = b_s).$$

In fact, in its most general form we have

$P(X$ satisfies condition Q_1; Y satisfies condition $Q_2)$
$= P(X$ satisfies condition $Q_1) . P(Y$ satisfies condition $Q_2)$.

9.1 Expectations

Given a function h, we may be interested in the average value taken by $h(X, Y)$. If $X = a_r$, $Y = b_s$, $h(X, Y)$ takes the value $h(a_r, b_s)$, and it takes it with probability $p_{r,s}$. We therefore consider the value $\sum_{r,s} h(a_r, b_s) p_{r,s}$ and call it the *expectation* of $h(X, Y)$. It is denoted by $E\{h(X, Y)\}$.

If h and k are two functions, $E\{h(X, Y) + k(X, Y)\}$

$$= \sum_{r,s} \{h(a_r, b_s) + k(a_r, b_s)\} p_{r,s}$$

9.1 THEORETICAL STATISTICS

$$= \sum_{r,s} h(a_r, b_s)p_{r,s} + \sum_{r,s} k(a_r, b_s)p_{r,s}$$
$$= E\{h(X, Y)\} + E\{k(X, Y)\}.$$

In other words, the expectation is additive.

We get the most striking example of this when

$$\left.\begin{array}{l} h(X, Y) = X \\ k(X, Y) = Y \end{array}\right\} \quad \text{(Admittedly special cases, but perfectly allowable.)}$$

Then, $E(X + Y) = E(X) + E(Y)$.

Some people doubt the truth of this. Others doubt the relevance saying there are some things you cannot add together like time and money—but you can! Suppose an actress is weighing up the relative merits of prospective rich husbands. The more money he has, the more she gets (let amount owned by a random suitor be X); the older he is, the shorter she has to wait to get it all (let age of random suitor be Y). Then to pick the best man she may give each a score represented by $X + Y$. What is the average score of the bunch? What our theory says is that we merely have to work out the average amount of capital over all suitors and add it to the average age.

This result is *always* true; it does *not* depend on any independence between X and Y. The expectation of the sum is always the sum of the expectations.

On the other hand, the relation

$$E(XY) = E(X).E(Y)$$

usually does depend on independence. It does not always depend on independence, for consider the bivariate distribution

$$P(X = -1; Y = 0) = \tfrac{1}{3},$$
$$P(X = 0; Y = 1) = \tfrac{1}{3},$$
$$P(X = 1; Y = 0) = \tfrac{1}{3}.$$

We can conveniently represent this distribution on graph paper (figure 9.1), putting equal 'blobs' of probability at the three points $(-1, 0)$, $(0, 1)$, $(1, 0)$.

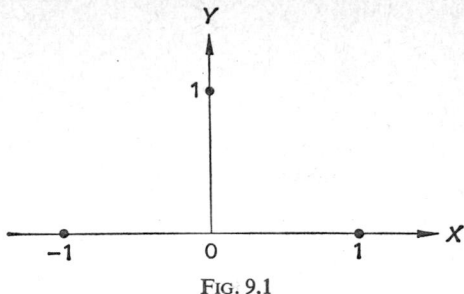

Fig. 9.1

Obviously, the random variables are dependent, for Y has to be 1 if X is 0. On the other hand,

$$E(X) = 0$$
$$E(Y) = 0.\tfrac{1}{3} + 1.\tfrac{1}{3} + 0.\tfrac{1}{3} = \tfrac{1}{3}$$
$$XY = 0 \text{ at all points.}$$

Therefore, $E(XY) = 0 = E(X).E(Y)$.

Summing up:

If X, Y are independent, $E(XY) = E(X).E(Y)$;

if $E(XY) = E(X).E(Y)$, X, Y *may not* be independent.

9.2 Moments

The generalisation of the moment in bivariate distributions is the *product moment*. It is defined by

$$\mu'_{i,j} = E(X^i Y^j).$$

Now $\mu'_{1,0} = E(X^1 Y^0)$
    $= E(X)$
    $=$ mean of X as if Y were not present at all.

Similarly $\mu'_{0,1} = E(Y)$
    $=$ mean of Y as if X were not present at all.

9.2 THEORETICAL STATISTICS

This enables us to define *moments about the mean* thus:
$$\mu_{i,j} = E\{(X - \mu'_{1,0})^i (Y - \mu'_{0,1})^j\}.$$

(i) $\mu_{0,0} = E(1) = 1$.

(ii) $\mu_{i,0} = E\{X - E(X)\}^i$
 = ith moment of X about its mean as if Y was not present.

Similarly, $\mu_{0,j} = j$th moment of Y about its mean.

(iii) $\mu_{2,0}$ = variance of X alone
$\mu_{0,2}$ = variance of Y alone.

So far, the results have been fairly trivial, because one of the suffices has been zero, thus effectively reducing the number of random variables from two to one. The three *quadratic-type* moments are $\mu_{2,0}$, $\mu_{0,2}$ (which are mentioned above) and $\mu_{1,1}$. This last is the first special case we have come across which is genuinely bivariate. It is *quadratic*, yet is not a variance. As it somehow combines X and Y, it is called the *covariance*. For its value we have

$$\begin{aligned}\mu_{1,1} &= E[\{X - E(X)\}.\{Y - E(Y)\}] \\ &= E\{XY - X.E(Y) - Y.E(X) + E(X).E(Y)\} \\ &= E(XY) - E(X).E(Y) - E(Y).E(X) + E(X).E(Y) \\ &= E(XY) - E(X).E(Y).\end{aligned}$$

One thing we notice immediately is that if X and Y are independent,
$$E(XY) = E(X).E(Y).$$
Therefore, the covariance of X and Y is zero.

This is one extreme; let us look at the other. The opposite of *independent* is *dependent*; and the strongest form of dependence is when Y is linear in X. A distribution for which $Y = X$ is given in figure 9.2.

Thus,
$$P(X = 0; Y = 0) = \tfrac{1}{3}$$
$$P(X = 1; Y = 1) = \tfrac{1}{3}$$
$$P(X = 2; Y = 2) = \tfrac{1}{3}.$$

DISCRETE BIVARIATE DISTRIBUTIONS

The values of XY are 0, 1, 4.

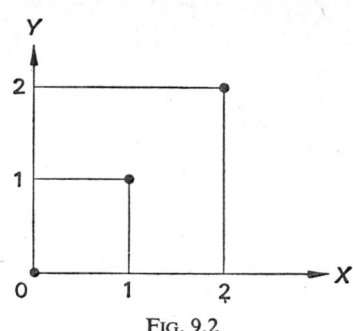

Fig. 9.2

Therefore,
$$E(XY) = \tfrac{5}{3}$$
$$E(X) = 1$$
$$E(Y) = 1.$$

Therefore, covariance $(X, Y) = E(XY) - E(X).E(Y)$
$$= \tfrac{5}{3} - 1 = \tfrac{2}{3}.$$

If we double the scale of Y, we get the distribution in figure 9.3,

given by
$$P(X = 0; Y = 0) = \tfrac{1}{3}$$
$$P(X = 1; Y = 2) = \tfrac{1}{3}$$
$$P(X = 2; Y = 4) = \tfrac{1}{3}.$$

The values of XY are now 0, 2, 8.

Therefore,
$$E(XY) = \tfrac{10}{3}$$
$$E(X) = 1$$
$$E(Y) = 2.$$

Therefore, the covariance of $(X, Y) = \tfrac{10}{3} - 1 \times 2$
$$= \tfrac{4}{3}.$$

Thus the covariance has doubled.

Now the covariance responds to the relationship between X and Y. If X and Y are independent, the covariance is zero. If X and Y lie

9.3 THEORETICAL STATISTICS

on a line of positive slope, the covariance is positive. If the slope of the line is increased, the covariance increases proportionately.

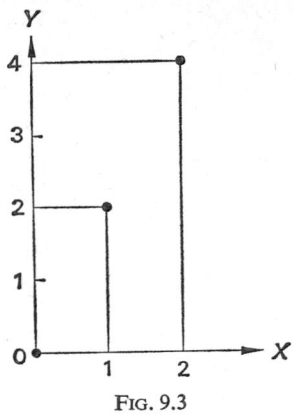

FIG. 9.3

In practice, the scale selected for Y could be a matter of indifference. The important thing could be the tightness of the relationship between X and Y; nothing could be tighter than linearity, whatever the slope. It would be convenient, therefore, if we had a measure which did not depend on the scale. When defining moments for single random variables we found we could introduce a new definition to off-set the effect of the origin. Can we do the same kind of thing with bivariate distributions to off-set the effect of scale?

9.3 Correlation

The answer to the question above is a modified form of the covariance called the *correlation coefficient*, defined by the relation:

$$\text{correlation } (X, Y) = \frac{\mu_{1,1}}{\sqrt{\mu_{2,0} \cdot \mu_{0,2}}}$$

It is usually denoted by ρ. The square root is always taken to be positive so the sign of ρ follows the sign of $\mu_{1,1}$.

DISCRETE BIVARIATE DISTRIBUTIONS 9.3

First let us establish the properties claimed for it.

(i) If U, V are random variables such that

$$\left.\begin{array}{l} U = aX + b \\ V = cY + d \end{array}\right\} \text{ where } a, b, c, d \text{ are constants,}$$

then $\quad E(U) = a \cdot (\text{mean of } X) + b$
$\quad\quad\quad\quad = a\mu'_{1,0} + b$
$\quad E(V) = c\mu'_{0,1} + d.$

Therefore,
covariance $(U, V) = E(aX + b - a\mu'_{1,0} - b) \times$
$\quad\quad\quad\quad\quad\quad\quad\quad\quad \times (cY + d - c\mu'_{0,1} - d)$
$\quad\quad\quad\quad\quad\quad = acE(X - \mu'_{1,0})(Y - \mu'_{0,1})$
$\quad\quad\quad\quad\quad\quad = ac\mu_{1,1}.$

(ii) correlation $(U, V) = \dfrac{\text{cov}(U, V)}{\sqrt{\text{var}(U) \cdot \text{var}(V)}}$

$\quad\quad\quad\quad\quad\quad\quad\quad = \dfrac{ac\mu_{1,1}}{\sqrt{a^2 \text{var}(X) \cdot c^2 \text{var}(Y)}}$

$\quad\quad\quad\quad\quad\quad\quad\quad = \dfrac{\mu_{1,1}}{\sqrt{\mu_{2,0} \cdot \mu_{0,2}}}$

$\quad\quad\quad\quad\quad\quad\quad\quad = \text{correlation } (X, Y).$

(iii) Hence, changing both the origin and the scale does not change the correlation between two random variables.

(iv) As a further property, if X and Y are independent, then

$$\text{correlation } (X, Y) = \dfrac{\mu_{1,1}}{\sqrt{\mu_{2,0} \cdot \mu_{0,2}}}$$

$$= 0 \text{ as } \mu_{1,1} = 0.$$

Thus if X, Y are independent, $\rho = 0$.

We have already suggested that the opposite extreme to *independent* is *linearly related*. In this case, any value for the random

9.3 THEORETICAL STATISTICS

variable X would automatically determine the value for the corresponding Y, and in fact
$$Y = mX + c.$$
Then
$$E(X) = \mu'_{1,0}$$
$$\text{variance } (X) = \mu_{2,0}$$
$$E(Y) = m\mu'_{1,0} + c$$
$$\text{variance } (Y) = m^2 \mu_{2,0}$$
$$\begin{aligned}
\text{covariance } (X, Y) &= E\{(X - \mu'_{1,0})(Y - m\mu'_{1,0} - c)\} \\
&= E\{(X - \mu'_{1,0})(mX - m\mu'_{1,0})\} \text{ as } Y = mX + c \\
&= mE(X - \mu'_{1,0})^2 \\
&= m\mu_{2,0}.
\end{aligned}$$

This will be positive if m is positive, and negative if m is negative.

Therefore, correlation $(X, Y) = \dfrac{\text{cov}(X, Y)}{\sqrt{\text{var}(X).\text{var}(Y)}}$

$$= \frac{m.\mu_{2,0}}{\sqrt{\mu_{2,0}.m^2\mu_{2,0}}}$$

$$= \frac{m\mu_{2,0}}{|m\mu_{2,0}|}$$

$$= +1 \text{ if } m > 0$$
$$= -1 \text{ if } m < 0.$$

The case $m = 0$ is artificial, for it means that Y is tied to a single value all the time. It is a random variable which does not vary! Therefore, we exclude horizontal lines from our consideration in this context. Vertical lines are already implicitly excluded, for we may not take $m = \infty$.

The more interesting question is the converse. What can we deduce from $\rho = 1$ (excluding the artificial cases)?

The artificial cases arise if X or Y is tied to single values, i.e. if

$\mu_{2,0} = 0$ or $\mu_{0,2} = 0$. Excluding these cases, both variances are positive.

Now
$$1 = \rho = \frac{\mu_{1,1}}{\sqrt{\mu_{2,0} \cdot \mu_{0,2}}}.$$

Therefore, $\quad \mu_{1,1} = +\sqrt{\mu_{2,0} \cdot \mu_{0,2}} > 0.$

Suppose
$$E(X) = u$$
$$E(Y) = v,$$

then, $\quad E\{(X-u)\sqrt{\mu_{0,2}/\mu_{2,0}} - (Y-v)\}^2$

$$= \frac{\mu_{0,2}}{\mu_{2,0}} E(X-u)^2 - 2\sqrt{\mu_{0,2}/\mu_{2,0}} E(X-u)(Y-v) + E(Y-v)^2$$

$$= \frac{\mu_{0,2}}{\mu_{2,0}} \cdot \mu_{2,0} - 2\sqrt{\mu_{0,2}/\mu_{2,0}} \cdot \mu_{1,1} + \mu_{0,2}$$

$$= \mu_{0,2} - 2\sqrt{\mu_{0,2}/\mu_{2,0}}\sqrt{\mu_{2,0} \cdot \mu_{0,2}} + \mu_{0,2}$$

$$= \mu_{0,2} - 2\mu_{0,2} + \mu_{0,2}$$

$$= 0.$$

Now if at any of the discrete 'blobs' of probability in the (X, Y) plane,

$$(X-u)\sqrt{\mu_{0,2}/\mu_{2,0}} - (Y-v) \neq 0,$$

the square of the value it takes will be positive, and so it will contribute a non-zero expectation. But the expectation is zero.

Therefore, $\quad (X-u)\sqrt{\mu_{0,2}/\mu_{2,0}} - (Y-v) = 0$

at all the discrete probability 'blobs'. Therefore, the 'blobs' lie on a line having equation

$$y - v = \sqrt{\mu_{0,2}/\mu_{2,0}}(x - u).$$

This is a line through the point (u, v) having slope

$$m = \sqrt{\mu_{0,2}/\mu_{2,0}} \quad \text{(positive)}.$$

9.3 THEORETICAL STATISTICS

Similarly if $\rho = -1$, we may show that the probability 'blobs' lie on a straight line of negative slope.

It only remains to show that $|\rho| = 1$ really is the extreme case; i.e. that there is no case for which $|\rho| > 1$. This is easily established, for if t is any number, then

$$E\{(X - u)t - (Y - v)\}^2, \text{ where } E(X) = u; E(Y) = v$$
$$= E(X - u)^2 . t^2 - 2E(X - u)(Y - v) . t + E(Y - v)^2$$
$$= \mu_{2,0} . t^2 - 2\mu_{1,1} . t + \mu_{0,2}.$$

But no matter what value t takes,

$$\{(X - u)t - (Y - v)\}^2 \geqslant 0$$

Therefore the expectation is positive or zero.

Therefore, $\quad \mu_{2,0} . t^2 - 2\mu_{1,1} . t + \mu_{0,2} \geqslant 0$ for all t.

Therefore, $\quad 4\mu^2_{1,1} \leqslant 4\mu_{2,0}\mu_{0,2}$ [This is similar to the condition for complex roots to a quadratic.]

Therefore, $$\rho^2 = \frac{\mu^2_{1,1}}{\mu_{2,0}\mu_{0,2}}$$
$$\leqslant 1.$$

Therefore, $\quad |\rho| \leqslant 1.$

Summing up:

- $-1 \leqslant \rho \leqslant 1$.
- $\rho = +1$ if and only if the probability points lie on a line of positive slope.
- $\rho = -1$ if and only if the probability points lie on a line of negative slope.
- If X, Y are independent, $\rho = 0$.
- If $\rho = 0$, X, Y need not be independent (for we have already had an example of dependent random variables having zero covariance, and hence zero correlation).

As we have the extreme values, we can use ρ as an absolute *measure of association* between two random variables. For $\rho = 0$, we say the random variables are uncorrelated. For $|\rho|$ approximately zero they are just correlated. For $|\rho|$ nearly 1, they are highly correlated. At this point, however, one must not let go of common sense or of relevant background experience. High correlations can and do occur in physics. But in psychology, where one is correlating marks in mathematics and in languages over a class of children, a correlation of ·9 is virtually unheard of. One might expect higher intelligence to produce higher marks in both; but there are so many cross-currents that a ρ of ·5 would, in a psychological context, be thought of as pretty high.

9.4 Correlation as a Measure of Association

If a class of N children takes a mathematics paper and a languages paper, and a random child has mathematics mark X and language mark Y, then X, Y are paired random variables from a discrete bivariate distribution. We can obtain the whole distribution by noting the pairs of marks over the whole class.

In this situation, we might be interested in knowing whether the language mark was linked to the mathematics mark; if it is, and the relationship is approximately linear, then ρ will be close to 1. If there is an inverse relationship, so that a higher mathematics mark means a lower language mark, then ρ will be close to -1. If on balance over the whole class there is little or no association, then ρ will be close to zero. Hence, ρ is a good measure of how performance in a language is linked with performance in mathematics.

If you get something useful here, you could go on and correlate mathematics with science, or languages with history. In this way you could get ideas about which pairs of subjects were positively related and which negatively (in the sense that a larger X is, on average, linked with a smaller Y). You could also examine the magnitudes of the correlation coefficients, and so see which pairs of subjects were most strongly linked and which least strongly.

9.5 Rank Correlation

The correlation coefficient ρ is sometimes referred to as the *product–moment correlation*, as it is derived from the product

9.5 THEORETICAL STATISTICS

moment $\mu_{1,1}$. But the name is also intended to distinguish it from other kinds of correlation coefficient such as Spearman's *rank correlation*, after the English psychologist C. E. Spearman (1863–1945). This arises if we do not have (or we discard) the precise mathematics and language marks, and rely purely on the final orders of the children in the two cases. In this case, the rank correlation is defined to be:

$$1 - \frac{6 \sum_{i}^{N} d^2_i}{N(N^2 - 1)}$$

where d_i is the difference in the ordered positions in mathematics and the language of the ith child in the class. This formula is usually presented right out of the blue; this is both unnecessary and misleading.

Suppose the children have identity numbers 1, 2, ... N, and that the ith child has mathematics position x_i and language position y_i; where, for simplicity, no two x's are equal, nor two y's.

If X, Y are the positions of a random child in mathematics and in the language, the bivariate distribution of (X, Y) is given by

$$P(X = x_i; Y = y_i) = \frac{1}{N} \quad i = 1, 2, \ldots N.$$

For this distribution, the *product-moment correlation* can be shown to be equal to

$$1 - \frac{6 \sum_{i}^{N} d^2_i}{N(N^2 - 1)} \ .$$

Hence, Spearman's rank correlation is not a different kind of correlation at all; it is the ordinary kind of product-moment correlation, but applied to the ordinal positions rather than to the marks themselves. It is a fair enough measure of association when the marks are not available; but no sensible person would use the marks merely to obtain the ordinal positions so as to obtain Spearman's

DISCRETE BIVARIATE DISTRIBUTIONS 9.6

coefficient, unless possibly he were lazy or without calculating devices. If you have to face up to a product-moment correlation in some form or other, it is better to have the form containing the maximum amount of information.

9.6 Sums of Independent Random Variables

If X is a random variable from a binomial distribution having parameters m, p, and Y is an independent random variable from a binomial distribution having parameters n, p,

then $P(X = r; Y = s) = P(X = r) \cdot P(X = s)$ by independence

$$= \binom{m}{r} p^r (1-p)^{m-r} \cdot \binom{n}{s} p^s (1-p)^{n-s}$$

$$= \binom{m}{r}\binom{n}{s} p^{r+s}(1-p)^{m+n-r-s}$$

where $r = 0, 1, 2 \ldots m$
where $s = 0, 1, 2 \ldots n$.

Thus we have expressed the two separate binomial distributions in terms of a single bivariate distribution.

Given the random value X, and the random value Y, we could be interested in the sum of the two values, that is in

$$Z = X + Y.$$

Clearly, Z is a random variable itself, so what we would want to know is the distribution of Z.

Tackling this in a straightforward way:

$$Z = 0 \text{ if } X = 0 \text{ and } Y = 0$$

$$Z = 1 \text{ if } X = 0 \text{ and } Y = 1$$
$$\text{or } X = 1 \text{ and } Y = 0$$

$$Z = 2 \text{ if } X = 0 \text{ and } Y = 2$$
$$\text{or } X = 1 \text{ and } Y = 1$$
$$\text{or } X = 2 \text{ and } Y = 0 \text{ etc.}$$

9.6 THEORETICAL STATISTICS

In particular, $Z = t$ if $X = 0$ and $Y = t$
or $X = 1$ and $Y = t - 1$
or $X = 2$ and $Y = t - 2$ etc.

Therefore,

$P(Z = t) = P(X = 0; Y = t) + P(X = 1; Y = t - 1) + \ldots$
(as the separate bivariate events are exclusive)

$$= \sum_{r=0}^{t} P(X = r; Y = t - r)$$

$$= \sum_{r=0}^{t} \binom{m}{r}\binom{n}{t-r} p^t (1-p)^{m+n-t} \quad \text{(from the bivariate distribution)}$$

$$= p^t (1-p)^{m+n-t} \sum_{r=0}^{t} \binom{m}{r}\binom{n}{t-r}.$$

To finish off this piece of work, we have to do some mathematics. Now it is not difficult to show that

$$\binom{m}{0}\binom{n}{t} + \binom{m}{1}\binom{n}{t-1} + \ldots + \binom{m}{t}\binom{n}{0} = \binom{m+n}{t},$$

although it does need correct interpretation when t is larger than m or n. We can, however, avoid all such workings by looking at the statistics of the situation.

We started with a random variable X having a binomial distribution with parameters m, p. How could this X have arisen? It could very well have arisen as the number of times an event E occurred in m independent trials when the probability of success in a single trial was p. Similarly for Y, only this time the parameters are n and p.

If we decide to take m (independent) trials therefore, we get X occurrences. If we change our minds and decide instead to take $m + n$ (independent) trials, we get a total of Z occurrences; and by past theory, Z has a binomial distribution with parameters $m + n$, p. But Z equals the number of occurrences in the first set plus the number in the additional set, that is

$$Z = X + Y,$$

Therefore, $X + Y$ has a binomial distribution with parameters $m + n, p$.

This is a simple example of how random variables can be added together, and of how to find the distribution of the sum. It can immediately be applied to the Poisson distribution; for if now X has a Poisson distribution with parameter m_1, it has approximately a binomial distribution with parameters m_1/p and p, where p is very small. Similarly, if Y has a Poisson distribution with parameter m_2 it has approximately a binomial distribution with parameter $m_2/p, p$. (Notice that the p is the same.) If now X and Y are given independent, $X + Y$ has approximately a binomial distribution with parameters $m_1/p + m_2/p, p$; therefore, it has approximately a Poisson distribution with parameter $m_1 + m_2$.

The approximations can be made as close as we like by making p sufficiently small. We need not doubt, therefore, that in the limit, $X + Y$ is accurately Poisson, though this is intuition at play (not to be despised) rather than mathematical rigour. Intuition is a fine 'labour-saving device'; also, it sometimes affords better insight into what is really at stake than pages of close mathematical reasoning. The only trouble is that it can sometimes play you false!

10. Random Sampling

10.1 Discrete Multivariate Distributions

A discrete distribution of a single random variable (sometimes called a *univariate distribution*) is concerned with 'blobs' of probability on a single axis. Thus, for a fair die we have equal 'blobs' at the points $x = 1, 2, 3, 4, 5, 6$. A discrete bivariate distribution is concerned with 'blobs' in a plane. A discrete multivariate distribution is concerned with 'blobs' in a space of many dimensions. It can be represented by the relations

$$P(X_1 = a_r; X_2 = b_s; \ldots; X_k = c_t) = p_{r,s,\ldots,t} \geqslant 0.$$

Complicated though this may look, it is not all that worse than for bivariate distributions. We have to change the notation to $X_1, X_2 \ldots, X_k$; for, if we began $X, Y, Z \ldots$, we would run out of letters.

The important case for us is when there is complete independence between all the random variables $X_1, X_2, \ldots, X_k$, i.e. when

$$P(X_1 = a_r; X_2 = b_s; \ldots; X_k = c_t)$$
$$= P(X_1 = a_r).P(X_2 = b_s) \ldots .P(X_k = c_t).$$

In this way, we can change our attention from the original multivariate distribution to the separate univariate distributions making it up. Conversely, we could have started with completely independent random variables $X_1, X_2 \ldots, X_k$, each with its own univariate distribution, and then compounded them to form a multivariate distribution. Whether we change over in this way is purely a matter of convenience—our convenience.

10.2 Random Samples

Given any discrete distribution

$$P(X = a_r) = p_r,$$

a random value from it is X. To avoid confusion, we shall call it X_1. Now a second random value from it can be denoted by X_2, and so forth. Finally, we might have X_n, so that in all we have the ordered sequence $(X_1, X_2, \ldots X_n)$. Each X here has the same distribution:

$$P(X_i = a_r) = p_r \quad i = 1, 2, \ldots, n.$$

If the X's are completely independent, we say that $(X_1, X_2, \ldots, X_n)$ is a *random sample* from the original discrete distribution.

Another way of looking at the situation is to say that a random sample is a kind of multivariate random variable. Given a single unknown X from a univariate distribution, we have a random *variable*. Given an ordered set of n completely independent X's from the univariate distribution we have a random *sample*.

In a concrete case, X_i is going to take a particular value, say x_i* $(i = 1, 2, \ldots, n)$. Thus, we shall have an ordered set of numbers $(x_1, x_2, \ldots, x_n)$. It is usual to call this a random sample also, though pedantically it would from our point of view be better to call it a sample which had been selected by random processes. The point is that there is nothing random about the particular value x_i; it is just one of the values from the set $\{a_1, a_2, a_3, \ldots\}$. The important thing is that while x_i is the value that it is, it could have been a_1 (with probability p_1) or a_2 (with probability p_2), and so forth. Which value it takes depends on chance, or random processes. If you throw a die and get a 1, then 1 is quite particular. But you were not bound to get the 1; you could have got 2 or 3 or 4 or 5 or 6. The 1 that you got was selected unpredictably from the set of all possible outcomes; also the selection of the 1 was not influenced by the outcomes of earlier throws, i.e. it was independent of them. In a word, therefore, the selection was random. To sum up, it is not any particular number which is random, but the method by which it was selected or obtained.

* x_i is called a *realisation of X_i*.

10.3 THEORETICAL STATISTICS

10.3 Sampling Statistics

If (X_1, X_2) is a sample of two from the die distribution

$$P(x = r) = \tfrac{1}{6}, \quad r = 1, 2, \ldots 6$$

X_1 can take any value from 1 to 6

X_2 can take any value from 1 to 6

hence, $X_1 + X_2$ can take any value from 2 to 12. Furthermore,

$$\begin{aligned} P(X_1 + X_2 = 2) &= P(X_1 = 1; X_2 = 1) \\ &= P(X_1 = 1).P(X_2 = 1) \text{ by independence} \\ &= \tfrac{1}{6}.\tfrac{1}{6} \\ &= \tfrac{1}{36}. \end{aligned}$$

Similarly,

$$\begin{aligned} P(X_1 + X_2 = 3) &= P(X_1 = 1; X_2 = 2) + P(X_1 = 2; X_2 = 1) \\ &= P(X_1 = 1).P(X_2 = 2) + P(X_1 = 2).P(X_2 = 1) \\ &= \tfrac{1}{36} + \tfrac{1}{36} \\ &= \tfrac{2}{36}. \end{aligned}$$

Continuing in this way, we can obtain the whole distribution of $X_1 + X_2$. In diagrammatic form it comes out as shown in figure 10.1.

We notice here that we get from the sample (X_1, X_2) to the expression $X_1 + X_2$ by the addition function. This is a particular case of the far more general function h given by

$$(X_1, X_2) \mapsto h(X_1, X_2).$$

This in turn is a particular case of the more general situation arising from samples of size n. In this case, we have

$$h: (X_1, X_2, \ldots, X_n) \mapsto h(X_1, X_2, \ldots, X_n).$$

Secondly we notice that $X_1 + X_2$ has a univariate distribution, and is itself a random variable. In general also, $h(X_1, X_2, \ldots, X_n)$ is

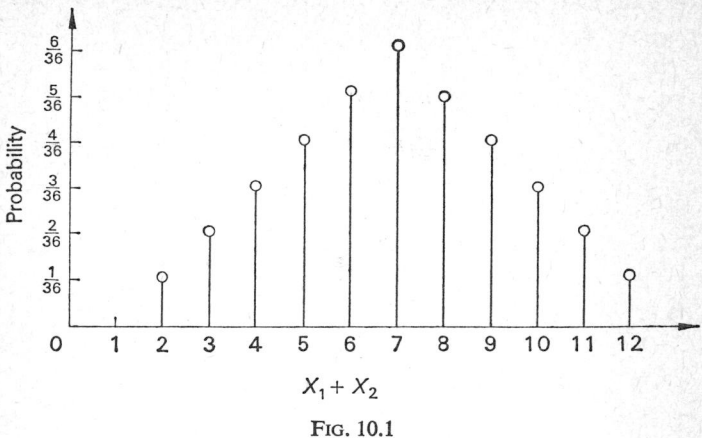

Fig. 10.1

a random variable with a univariate distribution. To reflect these ideas, we say that

> $h(X_1, X_2, \ldots, X_n)$ is a *sampling statistic*.

That it is called a 'statistic' scarcely calls for comment, except that the word is getting a trifle overloaded. The word 'sampling' is added to distinguish from earlier uses of the word 'statistic', and also to draw attention to the fact that $h(X_1, X_2, \ldots, X_n)$ is determined by the sample $(X_1, X_2, \ldots X_n)$.

Naturally enough, the distribution of $h(X_1, X_2, \ldots, X_n)$ is referred to as a *sampling distribution*. This distinguishes it from the distribution of the random variable X (in this context referred to as the *parent distribution*), and also draws attention to the fact that it is associated with a sampling statistic and hence with a sampling process.

A basic problem in the subject of mathematical statistics is to derive the sampling distribution of a sampling statistic given the

10.4 THEORETICAL STATISTICS

parent distribution. We cannot do this in general, except possibly in a symbolic form which does not tell us as much as we need to know.

10.4 Sampling Moments

If we cannot obtain the full sampling distribution of $Y = h(X_1, X_2, \ldots, X_n)$, we can often obtain the moments of the distribution; needless to say, these moments are called *sampling moments* to distinguish them from the moments of X. The first moment of Y given by $E(Y)$ is called the *sampling mean* of Y, and the second moment of Y called the *sampling variance* of Y. We shall consider what happens when Y is the mean or variance of the sample.

Just as

$$\frac{x_1 + x_2 + \ldots + x_n}{n} = \bar{x}$$

is called the *mean* of the set of the values $x_1, x_2, \ldots x_n$, so we say that

$$\frac{X_1 + X_2 + \ldots + X_n}{n} = \bar{X}$$

is the *mean* of the random variables $X_1, X_2, \ldots X_n$. In this latter case, we also say that $\bar{X}$ is the *mean* of the sample $(X_1, X_2, \ldots X_n)$ and we often denote it by m. Similarly,

$$\sum_{i=1}^{n} \frac{(X_i - \bar{X})^2}{n} = m_2$$

is called the *variance* of the sample.

$$E(m) = E\left(\frac{X_1 + X_2 + \ldots + X_n}{n}\right)$$

$$= \frac{1}{n} E(X_1 + X_2 + \ldots + X_n)$$

$$= \frac{1}{n}\{E(X_1) + E(X_2) + \ldots + E(X_n)\}.$$

But each of the random variables $X_1, X_2, \ldots X_n$ has the same parent distribution with mean μ (say).

Therefore,
$$E(m) = \frac{\mu + \mu + \ldots + \mu}{n}$$
$$= \frac{n\mu}{n} = \mu.$$

Let us think about the significance of this in plain English. In any particular case, we do not have the random sample $(X_1, X, \ldots, X_n)$ but the realisation of it $(x_1, x_2, \ldots, x_n)$. This realisation has mean $\bar{x}$. We could have got any number of different values for $\bar{x}$ if the realisation had come out different. But at least the average of all such values is equal to the distribution mean μ. In this average we count each value of $\bar{x}$ as often as it occurs; so if you like to express it thus, the average is a weighted average.

This is a comforting thought. We know that m need not equal μ. But $\bar{x}$ is one of a possible set of values whose central value *is* equal to μ. Thus it would be quite reasonable to take $\bar{x}$ as our estimate for an unknown distribution mean μ.

Notice the notation here. The mean of the distribution is denoted by the Greek letter μ. The mean of a sample from the distribution is denoted by the corresponding roman letter m. In a particular case, the realisation of m is $\bar{x}$. If μ is unknown, it is reasonable to estimate μ by our realisation of m.

The smaller the sampling variance of $\bar{X}$, the nearer any particular realisation $\bar{x}$ is likely to be to $E(\bar{X}) = \mu$ (because the whole distribution is less dispersed), and hence the better the estimate is likely to be. However, it would be interesting to see exactly how the relationship went.

First of all, it pays to work out $E(\bar{X}^2)$.
In the special case of $\mu = 0$ and $n = 2$,

$$E(\bar{X}^2) = E\left(\frac{X_1 + X_2}{2}\right)^2$$
$$= \tfrac{1}{4}E(X_1^2 + X_2^2 + 2X_1.X_2)$$

10.4 THEORETICAL STATISTICS

$$= \tfrac{1}{4}\{E(X_1{}^2) + E(X_2{}^2) + 2E(X_1.X_2)\}$$
$$= \tfrac{1}{4}\{\mu'_2 + \mu'_2 + 2E(X_1)E(X_2)\} \quad \text{by independence}$$
$$= \tfrac{1}{4}(2\mu'_2) \text{ as } E(X_1) = \mu = 0$$
$$= \frac{\mu_2}{2} \text{ as } \mu'_2 = \mu_2 \text{ for } \mu = 0.$$

For $n = 3$, we have

$$E(\bar{X}^2) = E\left(\frac{X_1 + X_2 + X_3}{3}\right)^2$$
$$= \tfrac{1}{9}E(X_1{}^2 + X_2{}^2 + X_3{}^2 + 2X_1X_2 + 2X_1X_3 + 2X_2X_3)$$
$$= \tfrac{1}{9}\{E(X_1{}^2) + E(X_2{}^2) + E(X_3{}^2)\}$$

(as the product terms have zero expectation for the same reason as before).

Therefore,
$$E(\bar{X}^2) = \tfrac{1}{9}(3\mu'_2)$$
$$= \frac{\mu_2}{3}.$$

It should by now be clear that for general n, and for $\mu = 0$,

$$E(\bar{X}^2) = \frac{\mu_2}{n}.$$

Indeed, you could provide a formal proof for yourself.

Now variance $(\bar{X}) = E(\bar{X} - \mu)^2$
$$= E(\bar{X}^2) - \mu^2$$
$$= E(\bar{X}^2) \quad (\text{as } \mu = 0 \text{ in our case})$$
$$= \frac{\mu_2}{n} \quad \text{as above.}$$

This result holds if $\mu = 0$. But any change of origin leaves variances unaltered, so that variance $(\bar{X})$ and μ_2 both remain constant. Hence we get the general relation

$$\text{variance } (\bar{X}) = \frac{1}{n} \cdot \text{variance } (X).$$

A more useful form of this relation in practice is

$$\text{standard deviation } (\bar{X}) = \frac{\sigma}{\sqrt{n}}.$$

This is obtained by taking the square root of both sides and remembering that $\mu_2 = \sigma^2$. This new relation suggests that one must quadruple the sample size to double the goodness of the estimate. This point is more useful in the context of continuous distributions, so we shall not bother to establish it rigorously here. But on common-sense grounds, and recalling how Tchebycheff's inequality is expressed in terms of σ, you should be able to accept the result without difficulty.

We have settled that

(i) $\bar{x}$ can be used as a reasonable estimate of an unknown μ.

(ii) $$\text{Variance } (\bar{X}) = \frac{\sigma^2}{n}.$$

We cannot work out (ii) however without having an estimate for $\sigma^2 = \mu_2$. Just as m is used to estimate μ, so it would look sensible to use m_2 to estimate μ_2. We therefore look at the sampling properties of m_2, assuming initially that $\mu = 0$.

$$E(m_2) = E\left\{\sum_{i=1}^{n} \frac{(X_i - \bar{X})^2}{n}\right\}$$
$$= \frac{1}{n} E\{\Sigma(X_i^2 - 2\bar{X}X_i + \bar{X}^2)\}$$

10.4 THEORETICAL STATISTICS

$$= \frac{1}{n} E\{\Sigma(X_i{}^2) - n\bar{X}^2\}$$

$$= \frac{1}{n}\left\{\sum_{i=1}^{n} E(X_i{}^2) - nE(\bar{X}^2)\right\}$$

$$= \frac{1}{n}(\mu_2 + \mu_2 + \ldots + \mu_2) - \frac{\mu_2}{n} \text{ as } \mu = 0$$

$$= \mu_2 - \frac{\mu_2}{n}$$

$$= \frac{n-1}{n}\mu_2.$$

This result holds for $\mu = 0$. As before, a change of origin leaves both sides of the equation unaltered. Therefore, it is generally true that

$$E(m_2) = \frac{n-1}{n}\mu_2.$$

The possible realisations of m_2 are therefore centred about $(n-1)\mu_2/n$, which is somewhat less than the μ_2 we are aiming for. We can easily correct for this, however, by changing to $nm_2/(n-1)$ in place of m_2. Thus our revised estimate for μ_2 is

$$\frac{n}{n-1} \frac{\Sigma(x_i - \bar{x})^2}{n} = \frac{\Sigma(x_i - \bar{x})^2}{n-1}.$$

This must be about the first case where intuition might have let us down.

Notation

It should be realised that for the work in these chapters, different writers employ different notations, depending in part on the main flavour of the book, and also (apparently) on nationality. We have been interested in the theory of the subject, therefore we have been interested more in the set of samples we might have got than in the particular sample we did get. Doing a physical experiment, we would get a particular sample of numerical values, but this would be only one of the possible samples we might have got. Therefore, we have defined a random sample in terms of random variables as $(X_1, X_2, \ldots, X_n)$. A set of numerical values $(x_1, x_2, \ldots, x_n)$ has then been a realisation of $(X_1, X_2, \ldots, X_n)$. Likewise,

$$m = \bar{X}, m_2 = \frac{\Sigma (X_i - \bar{X})^2}{n}$$

have been random variables. The advantages of this system are that

(i) We are compelled to consider the set of all sample readings we might have got, and not merely the particular sample readings we did get.
(ii) We can talk about the 'sampling distribution of the mean', the 'mean of the mean' and the 'variance of the mean'.

Other writers, more interested in applied statistics, will define a set of numerical readings $(x_1, x_2, \ldots, x_n)$ to be a random sample. This accords more with common practice. But we need not get bogged down in mere semantics. As long as we are clear in our own minds on the distinction between a random variable and its realisation, that is between $(X_1, X_2, \ldots, X_n)$ and $(x_1, x_2, \ldots, x_n)$, it does not matter too much how we fling the labels around *provided that we are consistent.*

Index

The numbers refer to pages

association, 77, 78

binomial coefficient, 22
binomial distribution, 59–61, 79–81
bivariate distribution, 43, 67–69, 72, 77–80, 82

conditional probability, 23–25, 44
continuous distribution, 89
correlation, 72–79
covariance, 70–74, 76
cumulative distribution function, 35–43, 67

die distribution, 58, 84
distribution (discrete), 45, 48, 49, 57–59, 67, 81

estimate, 87, 89, 90
events, 8, 14, 15, 19, 20
exclusive events, 17, 21, 29
exhaustive events, 27
expectations, 45, 46, 67, 68, 75, 76

independence, 25, 26, 29, 43, 44, 67–71, 73, 76, 79, 80, 82–84, 88

large numbers, 63
limits, 2–4, 6, 13, 39–41, 45, 46

mean, 48, 51, 52, 58, 64, 69, 86, 87, 91
moment generating function, 55, 57
moments, 47, 50, 57–59, 69, 72
moments about the mean, 49–51, 59, 70, 86
multivariate distribution, 44, 82

odds, 34

parameters, 59–61, 79–81

parent distribution, 85–87
Poisson distribution, 60–62, 81
probability, 1, 3–6, 10, 14–16, 19
probability model, 11–13
product moment, 69

random sample, 83, 86, 91
random sampling, 82
random sequences, 4–6, 13
random variable, 35, 36, 42, 59, 61, 65–67, 69, 72, 76, 77, 79–82, 84–87, 91
randomness, 5, 13, 14, 83
rank correlation, 77, 78
realisations, 83, 87, 90, 91
relative frequency, 2–6, 10, 13, 14, 63
rules of probability, 18, 20–23, 25, 27, 28, 37, 44

sample (see *random sample*)
sample space, 8, 14–16
sampling distribution, 85, 86, 91
sampling mean, 86
sampling moments, 86
sampling statistic, 84, 85
sampling variance, 86, 87
Spearman, C. E., 78
standard deviation, 50, 52, 89
stochastic limits, 65, 66

Tchebycheff, P. L. (inequality), 54, 65, 89
transformation, 51
trial, 11, 12, 20, 63

univariate distribution, 82, 84, 85

variance, 50, 52, 58, 64, 70, 74, 86, 88, 89, 91

weighted mean (average), 47, 87